GRIFFIN'S EGG

Also in Legend by Michael Swanwick

IN THE DRIFT
VACUUM FLOWERS

GRIFFIN'S EGG

Michael Swanwick

Illustrated by Peter Gudynas

CENTURY
A LEGEND NOVELLA
LONDON SYDNEY AUCKLAND JOHANNESBURG

A Legend Novella published by Century

First published in Great Britain in 1991 by
Random Century Group
20 Vauxhall Bridge Road, London SW1V 2SA

Century Hutchinson South Africa (Pty) Ltd
PO Box 337, Bergvlei 2012, South Africa

Random Century Australia Pty Ltd
20 Alfred Street, Milsons Point, Sydney, NSW 2061
Australia

Random Century New Zealand Ltd
PO BOX 40–086, Glenfield, Auckland 10
New Zealand

A CIP Catalogue Record for this book is available from
the British Library

ISBN 0 7126 4578 0 (hardcover) 0 7126 4577 2 (paperback)

Phototypeset by Input Typesetting Ltd, London

Printed and bound in Great Britain by
Mackays of Chatham PLC, Chatham, Kent

This book is dedicated to the Loud Philadelphians:

Tess Kissinger, Bob Walters, Susan Casper, Gardner Dozois, Marianne Porter, Mike Ford *emeritus*, Greg Frost, Joanne Burke, David Axler, Ray Ridenour (hon.), Tim Sullivan *emeritus*, and occasionally Janet and Karl Kofoed.

The moon? It is a griffin's egg,
Hatching to-morrow night.
And how the little boys will watch
With shouting and delight
To see him break the shell and stretch
And creep across the sky.
The boys will laugh. The little girls,
I fear, may hide and cry . . .

Vachel Lindsay

The sun cleared the mountains. Gunther Weil raised a hand in salute, then winced as the glare hit his eyes in the instant it took his helmet to polarize.

He was hauling fuel rods to Chatterjee Crater industrial park. The Chatterjee B reactor had gone critical forty hours before dawn, taking fifteen remotes and a microwave relay with it, and putting out a power surge that caused collateral damage to every factory in the park. Fortunately, the occasional meltdown was designed into the system. By the time the sun rose over the Rhaeticus highlands, a new reactor had been built and was ready to go on-line.

Gunther drove automatically, gauging his distance from Bootstrap by the amount of trash lining the Mare Vaporum road. Close by the city, discarded construction machinery and damaged assemblers sat in open-vacuum storage, awaiting possible salvage. Ten kilometres out, a pressurized van had exploded, scattering machine parts and giant worms of insulating foam across the landscape. At twenty-five kilometres, a poorly graded stretch of road had claimed any number of cargo skids and shattered running lights from passing traffic.

Forty kilometres out, though, the road was clear, a straight, clean gash in the dirt. Ignoring the voices at the back of his skull, the traffic chatter and automated safety messages that the truck routinely fed into his transceiver chip, he scrolled up the topographicals on the dash.

Right about here.

Gunther turned off the Mare Vaporum road and began laying tracks over virgin soil. 'You've left your prescheduled route,' the truck said. 'Deviations from schedule may only be made with the recorded permission of your dispatcher.'

9

'Yeah, well.' Gunther's voice seemed loud in his helmet, the only physical sound in a babel of ghosts. He'd left the cabin unpressurized, and the insulated layers of his suit stilled even the conduction rumbling from the treads. 'You and I both know that so long as I don't fall too far behind schedule, Beth Hamilton isn't going to care if I stray a little in between.'

'You have exceeded this unit's linguistic capabilities.'

'That's okay, don't let it bother you.' Deftly he tied down the send switch on the truck radio with a twist of wire. The voices in his head abruptly died. He was completely isolated now.

'You said you wouldn't do that again.' The words, broadcast directly to his trance chip, sounded as deep and resonant as the voice of God. 'Generation Five policy expressly requires that all drivers maintain constant radio—'

'Don't whine. It's unattractive.'

'You have exceeded this unit's linguistic—'

'Oh, shut up.' Gunther ran a finger over the topographical maps, tracing the course he'd plotted the night before: thirty kilometres over cherry soil, terrain no human or machine had ever crossed before, and then north on Murchison road. With luck he might even manage to be at Chatterjee early.

He drove into the lunar plain. Rocks sailed by to either side. Ahead, the mountains grew imperceptibly. Save for the treadmarks dwindling behind him, there was nothing from horizon to horizon to show that humanity had ever existed. The silence was perfect.

Gunther lived for moments like this. Entering that clean, desolate emptiness, he experienced a vast expansion of being, as if everything he saw, stars, plain, craters and all, were encompassed within himself. Bootstrap City was only a fading dream, a distant island on the gently rolling surface of a stone sea. Nobody will ever be first here again, he thought. Only me.

A memory floated up from his childhood. It was Christmas Eve and he was in his parents' car, on the way to midnight Mass. Snow was falling, thickly and windlessly, rendering all the familiar roads of Düsseldorf clean and pure under sheets of white. His father drove, and he himself leaned over the front seat to stare ahead in fascination into this peaceful, transformed world. The silence was perfect.

He felt touched by solitude and made holy.

The truck plowed through a rainbow of soft greys, submerged hues more hints than colours, as if something bright and festive held itself hidden just beneath a coating of dust. The sun was at his shoulder, and when he spun the front axle to avoid a boulder, the truck's shadow wheeled and reached for infinity. He drove reflexively, mesmerized by the austere beauty of the passing land.

At a thought, his peecee put music on his chip. 'Stormy Weather' filled the universe.

He was coming down a long, almost imperceptible slope when the controls went dead in his hands. The truck powered down and coasted to a stop. 'Goddamn you, you asshole machine!' he snarled. 'What is it this time?'

'The land ahead is impassable.'

Gunther slammed a fist on the dash, making the maps dance. The land ahead was smooth and sloping, any unruly tendencies tamed eons ago by the Mare Imbrium explosion. Sissy stuff. He kicked the door open and clambered down.

The truck had been stopped by a baby rille: a snake-like depression meandering across his intended route, looking for all the world like a dry streambed. He bounded to its edge. It was fifteen metres across, and three metres down at its deepest. Just shallow enough that it wouldn't show up on the topos. Gunther returned to the cab, slamming the door noiselessly behind him.

'Look. The sides aren't very steep. I've been down worse a hundred times. We'll just take it slow and easy, okay?'

'The land ahead is impassable,' the truck said. 'Please return to the originally scheduled course.'

Wagner was on now. *Tannhäuser*. Impatiently, he thought it off.

'If you're so damned heuristic, then why won't you ever listen to reason?' He chewed his lip angrily, gave a quick

11

shake of his head. 'No, going back would put us way off schedule. The rille is bound to peter out in a few hundred metres. Let's just follow it until it does, then angle back to Murchison. We'll be at the park in no time.'

Three hours later he finally hit the Murchison road. By then he was sweaty and smelly and his shoulders ached with tension. 'Where are we?' he asked sourly. Then, before the truck could answer, 'Cancel that.' The soil had turned suddenly black. That would be the ejecta fantail from the Sony-Reinpfaltz mine. Their railgun was oriented almost due south in order to avoid the client factories, and so their tailings hit the road first. That meant he was getting close.

Murchison was little more than a confluence of truck treads, a dirt track crudely levelled and marked by blazes of orange paint on nearby boulders. In quick order Gunther passed through a series of landmarks: Harada Industrial fantail, Sea of Storms Macrofacturing fantail, Krupp Fünfzig fantail. He knew them all. G5 did the robotics for the lot.

A light flatbed carrying a shipped bulldozer sped past him, kicking up a spray of dust that fell as fast as pebbles. The remote driving it waved a spindly arm in greeting. He waved back automatically, and wondered if it was anybody he knew.

The land hereabouts was hacked and gouged, dirt and boulders shoved into careless heaps and hills, the occasional tool station or Oxytank Emergency Storage Platform chopped into a nearby bluff. A sign floated by: TOILET FLUSHING FACILITIES ½ KILOMETRE. He made a face. Then he remembered that his radio was still off and slipped the loop of wire from it. Time to rejoin the real world. Immediately his dispatcher's voice, harsh and staticky, was relayed to his trance chip.

'—ofabitch! *Weil!* Where the fuck are you?'

'I'm right here, Beth. A little late, but right where I'm supposed to be.'

'Sonofa—' The recording shut off, and Hamilton's voice

12

came on, live and mean. 'You'd better have a real good explanation for this one, honey.'

'Oh, you know how it is.' Gunther looked away from the road, off into the dusty jade highlands. He'd like to climb up into them and never come back. Perhaps he would find caves. Perhaps there were monsters: vacuum trolls and moondragons with metabolisms slow and patient, taking centuries to move one body's-length, hyperdense beings that could swim through stone as if it were water. He pictured them diving, following lines of magnetic force deep, deep into veins of diamond and plutonium, heads back and singing. 'I picked up a hitchhiker, and we kind of got involved.'

'Try telling that to E. Izmailova. She's mad as hornets at you.'

'Who?'

'Izmailova. She's the new demolitions jock, shipped up here on a multicorporate contract. Took a hopper in almost four hours ago, and she's been waiting for you and Siegfried ever since. I take it you've never met her?'

'No.'

'Well, I have, and you'd better watch your step with her. She's exactly the kind of tough broad who won't be amused by your antics.'

'Aw, come on, she's just another tech on a retainer, right? Not in my line of command. It's not like she can do anything to me.'

'Dream on, babe. It wouldn't take much pull to get a fuck-up like you sent down to Earth.'

The sun was only a finger's-breadth over the highlands by the time Chatterjee A loomed into sight. Gunther glanced at it every now and then, apprehensively. With his visor adjusted to the H-alpha wavelength, it was a blazing white sphere covered with slowly churning black specks: more granular than usual. Sunspot activity seemed high. He wondered that the Radiation Forecast Facility hadn't posted a surface advisory. The guys at the Observatory were usually right on top of things.

13

Chatterjee A, B and C were a triad of simple craters just below Chladni, and while the smaller two were of minimal interest, Chatterjee A was the child of a meteor that had punched through the Imbrian basalts to as sweet a vein of aluminium ore as anything in the highlands. Being so convenient to Bootstrap made it one of management's darlings, and Gunther was not surprised to see that Kerr-McGee was going all out to get their reactor on-line again.

The park was crawling with walkers, stalkers and assemblers. They were all over the blister-domed factories, the smelteries, loading docks and vacuum garages. Constellations of blue sparks winked on and off as major industrial constructs were dismantled. Fleets of heavily loaded trucks fanned out into the lunar plain, churning up the dirt behind them. Fats Waller started to sing 'The Joint is Jumping' and Gunther laughed.

He slowed to a crawl, swung wide to avoid a gas-plater that was being wrangled on to a loader, and cut up the Chatterjee B ramp road. A new landing pad had been blasted from the rock just below the lip, and a cluster of people stood about a hopper resting there. One human and eight remotes.

One of the remotes was speaking, making choppy little gestures with its arms. Several stood inert, identical as so many antique telephones, unclaimed by Earthside management but available should more advisors need to be called on-line.

Gunther unstrapped Siegfried from the roof of the cab and, control pad in one hand and cable spool in the other, walked him towards the hopper.

The human strode out to meet him. 'You! What kept you?' E. Izmailova wore a jazzy red-and-orange Studio Volga boutique suit, in sharp contrast to his own company-issue suit with the G5 logo on the chest. He could not make out her face through the gold visor glass. But he could hear it in her voice: blazing eyes, thin lips.

'I had a flat tyre.' He found a good smooth chunk of rock and set down the cable spool, wriggling it to make sure it sat flush. 'We got maybe five hundred metres of shielded cable. That enough for you?'

A short, tense nod.

'Okay.' He unholstered his bolt gun. 'Stand back.' Kneeling, he anchored the spool to the rock. Then he ran a quick check of the unit's functions. 'Do we know what it's like in there?'

A remote came to life, stepped forward and identified himself as Don Sakai, of G5's crisis management team. Gunther had worked with him before: a decent enough guy, but like most Canadians he had an exaggerated fear of nuclear energy. 'Ms Lang here, of Sony-Reinpfaltz, walked her unit in but the radiation was so strong she lost control after a preliminary scan.' A second remote nodded confirmation, but the relay time to Toronto was just enough that Sakai missed it. 'The remote just kept on walking.' He coughed nervously, then added unnecessarily, 'The autonomous circuits were too sensitive.'

'Well, that's not going to be a problem with Siegfried. He's as dumb as a rock. On the evolutionary scale of machine intelligence he ranks closer to a crowbar than a computer.' Two and a half seconds passed, and then Sakai laughed politely. Gunther nodded to Izmailova. 'Walk me through this. Tell me what you want.'

Izmailova stepped to his side, their suits pressing together briefly as she jacked a patch cord into his control pad. Vague shapes flickered across the outside of her visor like the shadows of dreams. 'Does he know what he's doing?' she asked.

'Hey, I—'

'Shut up, Weil,' Hamilton growled on a private circuit. Openly, she said, 'He wouldn't be here if the company didn't have full confidence in his technical skills.'

'I'm sure there's never been any question—' Sakai began. He lapsed into silence as Hamilton's words belatedly reached him.

'There's a device on the hopper,' Izmailova said to Gunther. 'Go pick it up.'

He obeyed, reconfiguring Siegfried for a small, dense

15

load. The unit bent low over the hopper, wrapping large, sensitive hands about the device. Gunther applied gentle pressure. Nothing happened. Heavy little bugger. Slowly, carefully, he upped the power. Siegfried straightened.

'Up the road, then down inside.'

The reactor was unrecognizable, melted, twisted and folded in upon itself, a mound of slag with twisting pipes sprouting from the edges. There had been a coolant explosion early in the incident, and one wall of the crater was bright with sprayed metal. 'Where is the radioactive material?' Sakai asked. Even though he was a third of a million kilometres away, he sounded tense and apprehensive.

'It's all radioactive,' Izmailova said.

They waited. 'I mean, you know. The fuel rods?'

'Right now, your fuel rods are probably three hundred metres down and still going. We are talking about fissionable material that has achieved critical mass. Very early in the process the rods will have all melted together in a sort of superhot puddle capable of burning its way through rock. Picture it as a dense, heavy blob of wax slowly working its way towards the lunar core.'

'God, I love physics,' Gunther said.

Izmailova's helmet turned towards him, abruptly blank. After a long pause, it switched on again and turned away. 'The road down is clear at least. Take your unit all the way to the end. There's an exploratory shaft to one side there. Old one. I want to see if it's still open.'

'Will the one device be enough?' Sakai asked. 'To clean up the crater, I mean.'

The woman's attention was fixed on Siegfried's progress. In a distracted tone she said, 'Mr Sakai, putting a chain across the access road would be enough to clean up this site. The crater walls would shield anyone working nearby from the gamma radiation, and it would take no effort at all to reroute hopper overflights so their passengers would not be exposed. Most of the biological danger of a reactor meltdown comes from alpha radiation emitted by particulate radioisotopes in the air or water. When concentrated in the

body, alpha-emitters can do considerable damage; elsewhere, no. Alpha particles can be stopped by a sheet of paper. So long as you keep a reactor out of your ecosystem, it's as safe as any other large machine. Burying a destroyed reactor just because it is radioactive is unnecessary and, if you will forgive me for saying so, superstitious. But I don't make policy. I just blow things up.'

'Is this the shaft you're looking for?' Gunther asked.

'Yes. Walk it down to the bottom. It's not far.'

Gunther switched on Siegfried's chestlight, and sank a roller relay so the cable wouldn't snag. They went down. Finally Izmailova said, 'Stop. That's far enough.' He gently set the device down and then, at her direction, flicked the arming toggle. 'That's done,' Izmailova said. 'Bring your unit back. I've given you an hour to put some distance between the crater and yourself.' Gunther noticed that the remotes, on automatic, had already begun walking away.

'Um . . . I've still got fuel rods to load.'

'Not today you don't. The new reactor has been taken back apart and hauled out of the blasting zone.'

Gunther thought now of all the machinery being disassembled and removed from the industrial park, and was struck for the first time by the operation's sheer extravagance of scale. Normally only the most sensitive devices were removed from a blasting area. 'Wait a minute. Just what kind of monster explosive are you planning to *use*?'

There was a self-conscious cockiness to Izmailova's stance. 'Nothing I don't know how to handle. This is a diplomat-class device, the same design as saw action five years ago. Nearly one hundred individual applications without a single mechanical failure. That makes it the most reliable weapon in the history of warfare. You should feel privileged having the chance to work with one.'

Gunther felt his flesh turn to ice. 'Jesus Mother of God,' he said. 'You had me handling a briefcase nuke.'

'Better get used to it. Westinghouse Lunar is putting these little babies into mass production. We'll be cracking open mountains with them, blasting roads through the highlands, smashing apart the rille walls to see what's inside.'

18

Her voice took on a visionary tone. 'And that's just the beginning. There are plans for enrichment fields in Sinus Aestum. Explode a few bombs over the regolith, then extract plutonium from the dirt. We're going to be the fuel dump for the entire solar system.'

His dismay must have shown in his stance, for Izmailova laughed. 'Think of it as weapons for peace.'

'You should've been there!' Gunther said. 'It was unfucka-believable. The one side of the crater just disappeared. It dissolved into nothing. Smashed to dust. And for a real long time everything *glowed*! Craters, machines, everything. My visor was so close to overload it started flickering. I thought it was going to burn out. It was nuts.' He picked up his cards. 'Who dealt this mess?'

Krishna grinned shyly and ducked his head. 'I'm in.'

Hiro scowled down at his cards. 'I've just died and gone to Hell.'

'Trade you,' Anya said.

'No, I deserve to suffer.'

They were in Noguchi Park by the edge of the central lake, seated on artfully scattered boulders that had been carved to look water-eroded. A knee-high forest of baby birches grew to one side, and somebody's toy sailboat floated near the impact cone at the centre of the lake. Honeybees mazily browsed the clover.

'And then, just as the wall was crumbling, this crazy Russian bitch—'

Anya ditched a trey. 'Watch what you say about crazy Russian bitches.'

'—goes zooming up on her hopper . . .'

'I saw it on television,' Hiro said. 'We all did. It was news. This guy who works for Nissan told me the BBC gave it thirty seconds.' He'd broken his nose in karate practice, when he'd flinched into his instructor's punch, and the contrast of square white bandage with shaggy black eyebrows gave him a surly, piratical appearance.

Gunther discarded one. 'Hit me. Man, you didn't see anything. You didn't feel the ground shake afterwards.'

19

'Just what was Izmailova's connection with the Briefcase War?' Hiro asked. 'Obviously not a courier. Was she in the supply end or strategic?'

Gunther shrugged.

'You do remember the Briefcase War?' Hiro said sarcastically. 'Half of Earth's military elites taken out in a single day? The world pulled back from the brink of war by bold action? Suspected terrorists revealed as global heroes?'

Gunther remembered the Briefcase War quite well. He had been nineteen at the time, working on a Finlandia Geothermal project when the whole world had gone into spasm and very nearly destroyed itself. It had been a major factor in his decision to ship off the planet. 'Can't we ever talk about anything but politics? I'm sick and tired of hearing about Armageddon.'

'Hey, aren't you supposed to be meeting with Hamilton?' Anya asked suddenly.

He glanced up at the Earth. The east coast of South America was just crossing the dusk terminator. 'Oh, hell, there's enough time to play out the hand.'

Krishna won with three queens. The deal passed to Hiro. He shuffled quickly, and slapped the cards down with angry little punches of his arm. 'Okay,' Anya said, 'what's eating you?'

He looked up angrily, then down again and in a muffled voice, as if he had abruptly gone bashful as Krishna, said, 'I'm shipping home.'

'Home?'

'You mean to Earth?'

'Are you crazy? With everything about to go up in flames? *Why?*'

'Because I am so fucking tired of the Moon. It has to be the ugliest place in the universe.'

'Ugly?' Anya looked elaborately about at the terraced gardens, the streams that began at the top level and fell in eight misty waterfalls before reaching the central pond to be recirculated again, the gracefully winding pathways. People strolled through great looping rosebushes and past towers of forsythia with the dreamlike skimming stride that made

20

Moonwalking so like motion underwater. Others popped in and out of the office tunnels, paused to watch the finches loop and fly, tended to beds of cucumbers. At the midlevel straw market, the tents where off-duty hobby capitalists sold factory systems, grass baskets, orange glass paperweights and courses in postinterpretive dance and the meme analysis of Elizabethan poetry, were a jumble of brave silks, turquoise, scarlet and aquamarine. 'I think it looks nice. A little crowded, maybe, but that's the pioneer aesthetic.'

'It looks like a shopping mall, but that's not what I'm talking about. It's . . .' he groped for words. 'It's like – it's what we're doing to this world that bothers me. I mean, we're digging it up, scattering garbage about, ripping the mountains apart, and for what?'

'Money,' Anya said. 'Consumer goods, raw materials, a future for our children. What's wrong with that?'

'We're not building a future, we're building weapons.'

'There's not so much as a handgun on the Moon. It's an intercorporate development zone. Weapons are illegal here.'

'You know what I mean. All those bomber fuselages, detonation systems and missile casings that get built here and shipped to low Earth orbit. Let's not pretend we don't know what they're for.'

'So?' Anya said sweetly. 'We live in the real world, we're none of us naive enough to believe you can have governments without armies. Why is it worse that these things are being built here rather than elsewhere?'

'It's the short-sighted, egocentric greed of what we're doing that gripes me! Have you peeked out on the surface lately and seen the way it's being ripped open, torn apart and scattered about? There are still places where you can gaze upon a harsh beauty unchanged since the days our ancestors were swinging in trees. But we're trashing them. In a generation, two at most, there will be no more beauty to the Moon than there is to any other garbage dump.'

'You've seen what Earthbound manufacturing has done to the environment,' Anya said. 'Moving it off the planet is a good thing, right?'

'Yes, but the Moon—'

21

'Doesn't even *have* an ecosphere. There's nothing here to harm.'

They glared at each other. Finally Hiro said, 'I don't want to talk about it,' and sullenly picked up his cards.

Five or six hands later, a woman wandered up and plumped to the grass by Krishna's feet. Her eye shadow was vivid electric purple, and a crazy smile burned on her face. 'Oh hi,' Krishna said. 'Does everyone here know Sally Chang? She's a research component of the Centre for Self-Replicating Technologies, like me.'

The others nodded. Gunther said, 'Gunther Weil. Blue-collar component of Generation Five.'

She giggled.

Gunther blinked. 'You're certainly in a good mood.' He rapped the deck with his knuckles. 'I'll stand.'

'I'm on psilly,' she said.

'One card.'

'Psilocybin?' Gunther said. 'I might be interested in some of that. Did you grow it or microfacture it? I have a couple of factories back in my room; maybe I could divert one if you'd like to license the software?'

Sally Chang shook her head, laughing helplessly. Tears ran down her cheeks.

'Well, when you come down we can talk about it.' Gunther squinted at his cards. 'This would make a great hand for chess.'

'Nobody plays chess,' Hiro said scornfully. 'It's a game for computers.'

Gunther took the pot with two pair. He shuffled, Krishna declined the cut, and he began dealing out cards. 'So anyway, this crazy Russian lady—'

Out of nowhere, Chang howled. Wild gusts of laughter knocked her back on her heels and bent her forward again. The delight of discovery dancing in her eyes, she pointed a finger straight at Gunther. 'You're a robot!' she cried.

'Beg pardon?'

'You're nothing but a robot,' she repeated. 'You're a machine, an automaton. Look at yourself! Nothing but

22

stimulus-response. You have no free will at all. There's nothing there. You couldn't perform an original act to save your life.'

'Oh yeah?' Gunther glanced around, looking for inspiration. A little boy – it might be Pyotr Nahfees, though it was hard to tell from here – was by the edge of the water, feeding scraps of shrimp loaf to the carp. 'Suppose I pitched you into the lake? That would be an original act.'

Laughing, she shook her head. 'Typical primate behaviour. A perceived threat is met with a display of mock aggression.'

Gunther laughed.

'Then, when that fails, the primate falls back to a display of submission. Appeasement. The monkey demonstrates his harmlessness – you see?'

'Hey, this really isn't funny,' Gunther said warningly. 'In fact, it's kind of insulting.'

'And so back to a display of aggression.'

Gunther sighed and threw up both his hands. 'How am I supposed to react? According to you, anything I say or do is wrong.'

'Submission again. Back and forth, back and forth from aggression to submission and back again.' She pumped her arm as if it were a piston. 'Just like a little machine – you see? It's all automatic behaviour.'

'Hey, Kreesh – you're the neurobiowhatever here, right? Put in a good word for me. Get me out of this conversation.'

Krishna reddened. He would not meet Gunther's eyes. 'Ms Chang is very highly regarded at the Centre, you see. Anything she thinks about thinking is worth thinking about.' The woman watched him avidly, eyes glistening, pupils small. 'I think maybe what she means, though, is that we're all basically cruising through life. Like we're on autopilot. Not just you specifically, but all of us.' He appealed to her directly. 'Yes?'

'No, no, no, no.' She shook her head. 'Him specifically.'

'I give up.' Gunther put his cards down, and lay back on the granite slab so he could stare up through the roof glass at the waning Earth. When he closed his eyes, he could see

23

Izmailova's hopper, rising. It was a skimpy device, little more than a platform-and-chair atop a cluster of four bottles of waste-gas propellant, and a set of smart legs. He saw it lofting up as the explosion blossomed, seeming briefly to hover high over the crater, like a hawk atop a thermal. Hands by side, the red-suited figure sat, watching with what seemed inhuman calm. In the reflected light she burned as bright as a star. In an appalling way, she was beautiful.

Sally Chang hugged her knees, rocking back and forth. She laughed and laughed.

Beth Hamilton was wired for telepresence. She flipped up one lens when Gunther entered her office, but kept on moving her arms and legs. Dreamy little ghost motions that would be picked up and magnified in a factory somewhere over the horizon. 'You're late again,' she said with no particular emphasis.

Most people would have experienced at least a twinge of reality sickness dealing with two separate surrounds at once. Hamilton was one of the rare few who could split her awareness between two disparate realities without loss of efficiency in either. 'I called you in to discuss your future with Generation Five. Specifically, to discuss the possibility of your transfer to another plant.'

'You mean Earthside.'

'You see?' Hamilton said. 'You're not as stupid as you like to make yourself out to be.' She flipped the lens down again, stood very still, then lifted a metal-gauntleted hand and ran through a complex series of finger movements. 'Well?'

'Well what?'

'Tokyo, Berlin, Buenos Aires – do any of these hold magic for you? How about Toronto? The right move now could be a big boost to your career.'

'All I want is to stay here, do my job, and draw down my salary,' Gunther said carefully. 'I'm not looking for a shot at promotion, or a big raise, or a lateral career-track transfer. I'm happy right where I am.'

24

'You've sure got a funny way of showing it.' Hamilton powered down her gloves, and slipped her hands free. She scratched her nose. To one side stood her work table, a polished cube of black granite. Her peecee rested there, alongside a spray of copper crystals. At her thought, it put Izmailova's voice on to Gunther's chip.

'It is with deepest regret that I must alert you to the unprofessional behaviour of one of your personnel components,' it began. Listening to the complaint, Gunther experienced a totally unexpected twinge of distress and, more, of resentment that Izmailova had dared judge him so harshly. He was careful not to let it show.

'Irresponsible, insubordinate, careless, and possessed of a bad attitude.' He faked a grin. 'She doesn't seem to like me much.' Hamilton said nothing. 'But this isn't enough to . . .' His voice trailed off. 'Is it?'

'Normally, Weil, it would be. A demo jock isn't "just a tech on retainer", as you so quaintly put it; those government licences aren't easy to get. And you may not be aware of it, but you have very poor efficiency ratings to begin with. Lots of potential, no follow-through. Frankly, you've been a disappointment. However, lucky for you, this Izmailova dame humiliated Don Sakai, and he's let us know that we're under no particular pressure to accommodate her.'

'Izmailova humiliated Sakai?'

Hamilton stared at him. 'Weil, you're oblivious, you know that?'

Then he remembered Izmailova's rant on nuclear energy. 'Right, okay. I got it now.'

'So here's your choice. I can write up a reprimand, and it goes into your permanent file, along with Izmailova's complaint. Or you can take a lateral Earthside, and I'll see to it that these little things aren't logged into the corporate system.'

It wasn't much of a choice. But he put a good face on it. 'In that case it looks like you're stuck with me.'

'For the moment, Weil. For the moment.'

He was back on the surface the next two days running. The

first day he was once again hauling fuel rods to Chatterjee C. This time he kept to the road, and the reactor was refuelled exactly on schedule. The second day he went all the way out to Triesnecker to pick up some old rods that had been in temporary storage for six months while the Kerr-McGee people argued over whether they should be reprocessed or dumped. Not a bad deal for him, because although the sunspot cycle was on the wane, there was a surface advisory in effect and he was drawing hazardous-duty pay.

When he got there, a tech rep telepresenced in from somewhere in France to tell him to forget it. There'd been another meeting, and the decision had once again been delayed. He started back to Bootstrap with the new a cappella version of *The Threepenny Opera* playing in his head. It sounded awfully sweet and reedy for his tastes, but that was what they were listening to up home.

Fifteen kilometres down the road, the UV meter on the dash *jumped*.

Gunther reached out to tap the meter with his finger. It did not respond. With a freezing sensation at the back of his neck, he glanced up at the roof of the cab and whispered, 'Oh, no.'

'The Radiation Forecast Facility has just intensified its surface warning to a Most Drastic status,' the truck said calmly. 'This is due to an unanticipated flare storm, onset immediately. Everyone currently on the surface is to proceed with all haste to shelter. Repeat: Proceed immediately to shelter.'

'I'm eighty kilometres from—'

The truck was slowing to a stop. 'Because this unit is not hardened, excessive fortuitous radiation may cause it to malfunction. To ensure the continued safe operation of this vehicle, all controls will be frozen in manual mode and this unit will now shut off.'

With the release of the truck's masking functions, Gunther's head filled with overlapping voices. Static washed through them, making nonsense of what they were trying to say.

26

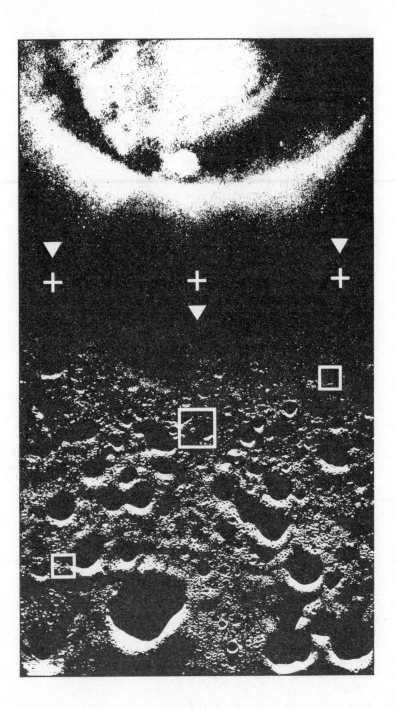

astic Status – *epeat: We***his is Beth. The****hail******yo****ere?*C
Su**ace adv***ry *as*******ve jus**issued****ost** om**on**good**uddy**ve
n up*******to Most**rast rastic ad*isory**Get off me a**oot**Miko, Sabra*
ic Sta**s. All unit* and the surfac*****ddamn**ou, Kangmei*****your asse**
personn*l are to find sh are you list***ng? Find undergrou***right now***
elter immediately. Maxim shelter. Don*t try to ge don't want*to hear you'**
um exposure twenty minut t back to Bootstrap. Too stayed behind to turn of
es. Repeat: Maximum exp far, it'll fry you. List f the lights. Who else
os*re twenty m*nutes. Fi en, ther* are thr*e facto is out*ther*? Come in ri
****helter im***iatel*** ries no****r from***ur pr ght n*w**Ev**yone! Anybo
Th******h***eco*ded*voi **ent**ocat*on**Are***u dy k*ow w**re*Mikhail is
ce of t***Radiati***Fore li***ning**y***goofoff*****C*mon, Misha***on't yo
cast Fa**lity, Due**o an**Weisskopf*AG*is one, Niss ***et coy on us***ound u
unpre**c*ed solar flar*******and**unar**acrostruct **your voice, hea***We g
th***urfa***adviso****as ural**Weil******me kn*****ot word Ezra's dug**nt**
****upgrad*****Most Dr if****'re listenin*****ome a factory out Chladn****

'Beth! The nearest shelter is back at Weisskopf – that's half
an hour at top speed and I've got an advisory here of twenty
minutes. Tell me what to do!'

But the first sleet of hard particles was coming in too
hard to make out anything more. A hand, his apparently,
floated forward and flicked off the radio relay. The voices
in his head died.

The crackling static went on and on. The truck sat
motionless, half an hour from nowhere, invisible death siz-
zling and popping down through the cab roof. He put
his helmet and gloves on, double-checked their seals, and
unlatched the door.

It slammed open. Pages from the op manual flew away,
and a glove went tumbling gaily across the surface, chasing
the pink fuzzy dice that Eurydice had given him that last
night in Sweden. A handful of wheat biscuits in an open
tin on the dash turned to powder and were gone, drawing
the tin after them. Explosive decompression. He'd forgotten
to depressurize. Gunther froze in dismayed astonishment
at having made so basic – so dangerous – a mistake.

Then he was on the surface, head tilted back, staring up
at the sun. It was angry with sunspots, and one enormous
and unpredicted solar flare.

I'm going to die, he thought.

For a long, paralysing instant, he tasted the chill certainty
of that thought. He was going to die. He knew that for a

28

fact, knew it more surely than he had ever known anything before.

In his mind, he could see Death sweeping across the lunar plain towards him. Death was a black wall, featureless, that stretched to infinity in every direction. It sliced the universe in half. On this side were life, warmth, craters and flowers, dreams, mining robots, thought, everything that Gunther knew or could imagine. On the other side. . . Something? Nothing? The wall gave no hint. It was unreadable, enigmatic, absolute. But it was bearing down on him. It was so close now that he could almost reach out and touch it. Soon it would be here. He would pass through, and then he would know.

With a start he broke free of that thought, and jumped for the cab. He scrabbled up its side. His trance chip hissing, rattling and crackling, he yanked the magnetic straps holding Siegfried in place, grabbed the spool and control pad, and jumped over the edge.

He landed jarringly, fell to his knees, and rolled under the trailer. There was enough shielding wrapped around the fuel rods to stop any amount of hard radiation – no matter what its source. It would shelter him as well from the sun as from his cargo. The trance chip fell silent, and he felt his jaws relaxing from a clenched tension.

Safe.

It was dark beneath the trailer, and he had time to think. Even kicking his rebreather up to full, and offlining all his suit peripherals, he didn't have enough oxygen to sit out the storm. So okay. He had to get to a shelter. Weisskopf was closest, only fifteen kilometres away, and there was a shelter in the G5 assembly plant there. That would be his goal.

Working by feel, he found the steel supporting struts, and used Siegfried's magnetic straps to attach himself to the underside of the trailer. It was clumsy, difficult work, but at last he hung face-down over the road. He fingered the walker's controls, and sat Siegfried up.

Twelve excruciating minutes later, he finally managed to get Siegfried down from the roof unbroken. The interior

29

wasn't intended to hold anything half so big. To get the walker in he had first to cut the door free, and then rip the chair out of the cab. Discarding both items by the roadside, he squeezed Siegfried in. The walker bent over double, reconfigured, reconfigured again, and finally managed to fit itself into the space. Gently, delicately, Siegfried took the controls and shifted into first.

With a bump, the truck started to move.

It was a hellish trip. The truck, never fast to begin with, wallowed down the road like a cast-iron pig. Siegfried's optics were bent over the controls, and couldn't be raised without jerking the walker's hands free. He couldn't look ahead without stopping the truck first.

He navigated by watching the road pass under him. To a crude degree he could align the truck with the treadmarks scrolling by. Whenever he wandered off the track, he worked Siegfried's hand controls to veer the truck back, so that it drifted slowly from side to side, zig-zagging its way down the road.

Shadows bumping and leaping, the road flowed towards Gunther with dangerous monotony. He jiggled and vibrated in his makeshift sling. After a while his neck hurt with the effort of holding his head back to watch the glaring road disappearing into shadow by the front axle, and his eyes ached from the crawling repetitiveness of what they saw.

The truck kicked up dust in passing, and the smaller particles carried enough of a static charge to cling to his suit. At irregular intervals he swiped at the fine grey film on his visor with his glove, smearing it into long, thin streaks.

He began to hallucinate. They were mild visuals, oblong patches of coloured light that moved in his vision and went away when he shook his head and firmly closed his eyes for a concentrated moment. But every moment's release from the pressure of vision tempted him to keep his eyes closed longer, and that he could not afford to do.

It put him in mind of the last time he had seen his mother, and what she had said then. That the worst part of being a widow was that every day her life began anew, no better than the day before, the pain still fresh, her husband's absence a physical fact she was no closer to accepting than ever. It was like being dead, she said, in that nothing ever changed.

Ah God, he thought, this isn't worth doing. Then a rock the size of his head came bounding towards his helmet. Frantic hands jerked at the controls, and Siegfried skewed the truck wildly, so that the rock jumped away and missed him. Which put an end to *that* line of thought.

He cued his peecee. 'Saint James' Infirmary' came on. It didn't help.

Come on, you bastard, he thought. You can do it. His arms and shoulders ached, and his back too, when he gave it any thought. Perversely enough, one of his legs had gone to sleep. At the angle he had to hold his head to watch the road, his mouth tended to hang open. After a while, a quivering motion alerted him that a small puddle of saliva had gathered in the curve of his faceplate. He was drooling. He closed his mouth, swallowing back his spit, and stared forward. A minute later he found that he was doing it again.

Slowly, miserably, he drove towards Weisskopf.

The G5 Weisskopf plant was typical of its kind: a white blister-dome to moderate temperature swings over the long lunar day, a microwave relay tower to bring in supervisory presence, and a hundred semiautonomous units to do the work.

Gunther overshot the access road, wheeled back to catch it, and ran the truck right up to the side of the factory. He had Siegfried switch off the engine, and then let the control pad fall to the ground. For well over a minute he simply hung there, eyes closed, savouring the end of motion. Then he kicked free of the straps, and crawled out from under the trailer.

Static scatting and stuttering inside his head, he stumbled into the factory.

In the muted light that filtered through the dome covering, the factory was dim as an undersea cavern. His helmet light seemed to distort as much as it illumined. Machines loomed

31

closer in the centre of its glare, swelling up as if seen through a fish-eye lens. He turned it off, and waited for his eyes to adjust.

After a bit, he could see the robot assemblers, slender as ghosts, moving with unearthly delicacy. The flare storm had activated them. They swayed like seaweed, lightly out of sync with each other. Arms raised, they danced in time to random radio input.

On the assembly lines lay the remains of half-built robots, looking flayed and eviscerated. Their careful frettings of copper and silver nerves had been exposed to view and randomly operated upon. A long arm jointed down, electric fire at its tip, and made a metal torso twitch.

They were blind mechanisms, most of them, powerful things bolted to the floor in assembly logic paths. But there were mobile units as well, overseers and jacks-of-all-trades, weaving drunkenly through the factory with sun-maddened eye.

A sudden motion made Gunther turn just in time to see a metal puncher swivel towards him, slam down an enormous arm and put a hole in the floor by his feet. He felt the shock through his soles.

He danced back. The machine followed him, the diamond-tipped punch sliding nervously in and out of its sheath, its movements as trembling and dainty as a newborn colt's.

'Easy there, baby,' Gunther whispered. To the far end of the factory, green arrows supergraffixed on the crater wall pointed to an iron door. The shelter. Gunther backed away from the punch, edging into a service aisle between two rows of machines that rippled like grass in the wind.

The punch press rolled forward on its trundle. Then, confused by that field of motion, it stopped, hesitantly scanning the ranks of robots. Gunther froze.

At last, slowly, lumberingly, the metal puncher turned away.

Gunther ran. Static roared in his head. Grey shadows swam among the distant machines, like sharks, sometimes coming closer, sometimes receding. The static loudened.

Up and down the factory, welding arcs winked on at the assembler tips, like tiny stars. Ducking, running, spinning, he reached the shelter and seized the airlock door. Even through his glove, the handle felt cold.

He turned it.

The airlock was small and round. He squeezed through the door and fit himself into the inadequate space within, making himself as small as possible. He yanked the door shut.

Darkness.

He switched his helmet lamp back on. The reflected glare slammed at his eyes, far too intense for such a confined area. Folded knees-to-chin into the roundness of the lock, he felt a wry comradeship with Siegfried back in the truck.

The inner lock controls were simplicity itself. The door hinged inward, so that air pressure held it shut. There was a yank bar which, when pulled, would bleed oxygen into the airlock. When pressure equalized, the inner door would open easily. He yanked the bar.

The floor vibrated as something heavy went by.

The shelter was small, just large enough to hold a cot, a chemical toilet and a rebreather with spare oxytanks. A single overhead unit provided light and heat. For comfort there was a blanket. For amusement, there were pocket-sized editions of the Bible and the Koran, placed there by impossibly distant missionary societies. Even empty, there was not much space in the shelter.

It wasn't empty.

A woman, frowning and holding up a protective hand, cringed from his helmet lamp. 'Turn that thing off,' she said.

He obeyed. In the soft light that ensued he saw: strack white flattop, pink scalp visible through the sides. High cheekbones. Eyelids lifted slightly, like wings, by carefully sculpted eye shadow. Dark lips, full mouth. He had to admire the character it took to make up a face so carefully, only to hide it beneath a helmet. Then he saw her red and orange Studio Volga suit.

It was Izmailova.

To cover his embarrassment, he took his time removing his gloves and helmet. Izmailova moved her own helmet from the cot to make room, and he sat down beside her. Extending a hand, he stiffly said, 'We've met before. My name is—'

'I know. It's written on your suit.'

'Oh yeah. Right.'

For an uncomfortably long moment, neither spoke. At last Izmailova cleared her throat and briskly said, 'This is ridiculous. There's no reason we should—'

CLANG

Their heads jerked towards the door in unison. The sound was harsh, loud, metallic. Gunther slammed his helmet on, grabbed for his gloves. Izmailova, also suiting up as rapidly as she could, tensely subvocalized into her trance chip: 'What is it?'

Methodically snapping his wrist latches shut one by one, Gunther said, 'I think it's a metal punch.' Then, because the helmet muffled his words, he repeated them over the chip.

CLANG. This second time, they were waiting for the sound. Now there could be no doubt. Something was trying to break open the outer airlock door.

'A what?!'

'Might be a hammer of some type, or a blacksmith unit. Just be thankful it's not a laser jig.' He held up his hands before him. 'Give me a safety check.'

She turned his wrists one way, back, took his helmet in her hands and gave it a twist to test its seal. 'You pass.' She held up her own wrists. 'But what is it trying to do?'

Her gloves were sealed perfectly. One helmet dog had a bit of give in it, but not enough to breach integrity. He shrugged. 'It's deranged – it could want anything. It might even be trying to repair a weak hinge.'

CLANG

'It's trying to get in here!'

'That's another possibility, yes.'

Izmailova's voice rose slightly. 'But even scrambled, there

34

can't possibly be any programs in its memory to make it do that. How can random input make it act this way?'

'It doesn't work like that. You're thinking of the kind of robotics they had when you were a kid. These units are state of the art: they don't manipulate instructions, they manipulate concepts. See, that makes them more flexible. You don't have to program in every little step when you want one to do something new. You just give it a goal—'

CLANG

'—like, to Disassemble a Rotary Drill. It's got a bank of available skills, like Cutting and Unbolting and Gross Manipulation, which it then fits together in various configurations until it has a path that will bring it to the goal.' He was talking for the sake of talking now, talking to keep himself from panic. 'Which normally works out fine. But when one of these things malfunctions, it does so on the conceptual level. See? So that—'

'So that it decides we're rotary drills that need to be disassembled.'

'Uh . . . yeah.'

CLANG

'So what do we do when it gets in here?' They had both involuntarily risen to their feet, and stood facing the door. There was not much space, and what little there was they filled. Gunther was acutely aware that there was not enough room here to either fight or flee.

'I don't know about you,' he said, 'but I'm going to hit that sucker over the head with the toilet.'

She turned to look at him.

CLA— The noise was cut in half by a breathy, whooshing explosion. Abrupt, total silence. 'It's through the outer door,' Gunther said flatly.

They waited.

Much later, Izmailova said, 'Is it possible it's gone away?'

'I don't know.' Gunther undogged his helmet, knelt and put an ear to the floor. The stone was almost painfully cold. 'Maybe the explosion damaged it.' He could hear the faint vibrations of the assemblers, the heavier rumblings of machines roving the factory floor. None of it sounded close.

35

He silently counted to a hundred. Nothing. He counted to a hundred again.

Finally he straightened. 'It's gone.'

They both sat down. Izmailova took off her helmet, and Gunther clumsily began undoing his gloves. He fumbled at the latches. 'Look at me.' He laughed shakily. 'I'm all thumbs. I can't even handle this, I'm so unnerved.'

'Let me help you with that.' Izmailova flipped up the latches, tugged at his glove. It came free. 'Where's your other hand?'

Then, somehow, they were each removing the other's suit, tugging at the latches, undoing the seals. They began slowly but sped up with each latch undogged, until they were yanking and pulling with frantic haste. Gunther opened up the front of Izmailova's suit, revealing a red silk camisole. He slid his hands beneath it, and pushed the cloth up over her breasts. Her nipples were hard. He let her breasts fill his hands and squeezed.

Izmailova made a low, groaning sound in the back of her throat. She had Gunther's suit open. Now she pushed down his leggings and reached within to seize his cock. He was already erect. She tugged it out and impatiently shoved him down on the cot. Then she was kneeling on top of him, and guiding him inside her.

Her mouth met his, warm and moist.

Half in and half out of their suits, they made love. Gunther managed to struggle one arm free, and reached within Izmailova's suit to run a hand up her long back and over the back of her head. The short hairs of her buzz cut stung and tickled his palm.

She rode him roughly, her flesh slippery with sweat against his. 'Are you coming yet?' she murmured. 'Are you coming yet? Tell me when you're about to come.' She bit his shoulder, the side of his neck, his chin, his lower lip. Her nails dug into his flesh.

'Now,' he whispered. Possibly he only subvocalized it, and she caught it on her trance chip. But then she clutched him tighter than ever, as if she were trying to crack his ribs, and her whole body shuddered with orgasm. Then he came

36

too, riding her passion down into spiralling desperation, ecstasy and release.

It was better than anything he had ever experienced before.

Afterwards, they finally kicked free of their suits. They shoved and pushed the things off the cot. Gunther pulled the blanket out from beneath them, and with Izmailova's help wrapped it about the both of them. They lay together, relaxed, not speaking.

He listened to her breathe for a while. The noise was soft. When she turned her face towards him, he could feel it, a warm little tickle in the hollow of his throat. The smell of her permeated the room. This stranger beside him.

Gunther felt weary, warm, at ease. 'How long have you been here?' he asked. 'Not here in the shelter, I mean, but . . .'

'Five days.'

'That little.' He smiled. 'Welcome to the Moon, Ms Izmailova.'

'Ekatarina,' she said sleepily. 'Call me Ekatarina.'

Whooping, they soared high and south, over Herschel. The Ptolemaeus road bent and doubled below them, winding out of sight, always returning. 'This is great!' Hiro crowed. 'This is – I should've talked you into taking me out here a year ago.'

Gunther checked his bearings and throttled down, sinking eastward. The other two hoppers, slaved to his own, followed in tight formation. Two days had passed since the flare storm and Gunther, still on mandatory recoop, had promised to guide his friends into the highlands as soon as the surface advisory was dropped. 'We're coming in now. Better triple-check your safety harnesses. You doing okay back there, Kreesh?'

'I am quite comfortable, yes.'

Then they were down on the Seething Bay Company landing pad.

Hiro was the second down and the first on the surface. He bounded about like a collie off its leash, chasing upslope

37

and down, looking for new vantage points. 'I can't believe I'm here! I work out this way every day, but you know what? This is the first time I've actually been out here. Physically, I mean.'

'Watch your footing,' Gunther warned. 'This isn't like telepresence – if you break a leg, it'll be up to Krishna and me to carry you out.'

'I trust you. Man, anybody who can get caught out in a flare storm, and end up nailing—'

'Hey, watch your language, okay?'

'Everybody's heard the story. I mean, we all thought you were dead, and then they found the two of you *asleep.* They'll be talking about it a hundred years from now.' Hiro was practically choking on his laughter. 'You're a legend!'

'Just give it a rest.' To change the subject, Gunther said, 'I can't believe you want to take a photo of this mess.' The Seething Bay operation was a strip mine. Robot bulldozers scooped up the regolith and fed it to a processing plant that rested on enormous skids. They were after the thorium here, and the output was small enough that it could be transported to the breeder reactor by hopper. There was no need for a railgun, and the tailings were piled in artificial mountains in the wake of the factory.

'Don't be ridiculous.' Hiro swept an arm southward, towards Ptolemaeus. 'There!' The crater wall caught the sun, while the lowest parts of the surrounding land were still in shadow. The gentle slopes seemed to tower; the crater itself was a cathedral, blazing white.

'Where is your camera?' Krishna asked.

'Don't need one. I'll just take the data down on my helmet.'

'I'm not too clear on this mosaic project of yours,' Gunther said. 'Explain to me one more time how it's supposed to work.'

'Anya came up with it. She's renting an assembler to cut hexagonal floor tiles in black, white and fourteen intermediate shades of grey. I provide the pictures. We choose the one we like best, scan it in black and white, screen for values of intensity, and then have the assembler lay the floor, one tile per pixel. It'll look great – come by tomorrow and see.'

'Yeah, I'll do that.'

Chattering like a squirrel, Hiro led them away from the edge of the mine. They bounded westward, across the slope.

Krishna's voice came over Gunther's trance chip. It was an old ground-rat trick. The chips had an effective transmission radius of fifteen metres – you could turn off the radio and talk chip-to-chip, if you were close enough. 'You sound troubled, my friend.'

He listened for a second carrier tone, heard nothing. Hiro was out of range. 'It's Izmailova. I sort of—'

'Fell in love with her.'

'How'd you know that?'

They were spaced out across the rising slope, Hiro in the lead. For a time neither spoke. There was a calm, confidential quality to that shared silence, like the anonymous stillness of the confessional. 'Please don't take this wrong,' Krishna said.

'Take what wrong?'

'Gunther, if you take two sexually compatible people, place them in close proximity, isolate them and scare the hell out of them, they will fall in love. That's a given. It's a survival mechanism, something that was wired into your basic make-up long before you were born. When billions of years of evolution say it's bonding time, your brain doesn't have much choice but to obey.'

'Hey, come on over here!' Hiro cried over the radio. 'You've got to see this.'

'We're coming,' Gunther said. Then, over his chip, 'You make me out to be one of Sally Chang's machines.'

'In some ways we *are* machines. That's not so bad. We feel thirsty when we need water, adrenalin pumps into the bloodstream when we need an extra boost of aggressive energy. You can't fight your own nature. What would be the point of it?'

'Yeah, but . . .'

'Is this great or what?' Hiro was clambering over a boulder field. 'It just goes on and on. And look up there!'

39

Upslope, they saw that what they were climbing over was the spillage from a narrow cleft entirely filled with boulders. They were huge, as big as hoppers, some of them large as prefab oxysheds. 'Hey, Krishna, I've been meaning to ask you – just what is it that you do out there at the Centre?'

'I can't talk about it.'

'Aw, come on.' Hiro lifted a rock the size of his head to his shoulder and shoved it away, like a shot-putter. The rock soared slowly, landed far downslope in a white explosion of dust. 'You're among friends here. You can trust us.'

Krishna shook his head. Sunlight flashed from the visor. 'You don't know what you're asking.'

Hiro hoisted a second rock, bigger than the first. Gunther knew him in this mood, nasty-faced and grinning. 'My point exactly. The two of us know zip about neurobiology. You could spend the next ten hours lecturing us, and we couldn't catch enough to compromise security.' Another burst of dust.

'You don't understand. The Centre for Self-Replicating Technologies is here for a reason. The lab work could be done back on Earth for a fraction of what a lunar facility costs. Our sponsors only move projects here that they're genuinely afraid of.'

'So what *can* you tell us about? Just the open stuff, the video magazine stuff. Nothing secret.'

'Well . . . okay.' Now it was Krishna's turn. He picked up a small rock, wound up like a baseball player and threw. It dwindled and disappeared in the distance. A puff of white sprouted from the surface. 'You know Sally Chang? She has just finished mapping the neurotransmitter functions.'

They waited. When Krishna added nothing further, Hiro dryly said, 'Wow.'

'Details, Kreesh. Some of us aren't so fast to see the universe in a grain of sand as you are.'

'It should be obvious. We've had a complete genetic map of the brain for almost a decade. Now add to that Sally Chang's chemical map, and it's analogous to being given the keys to the library. No, better than that. Imagine that you've spent your entire life within an enormous library

40

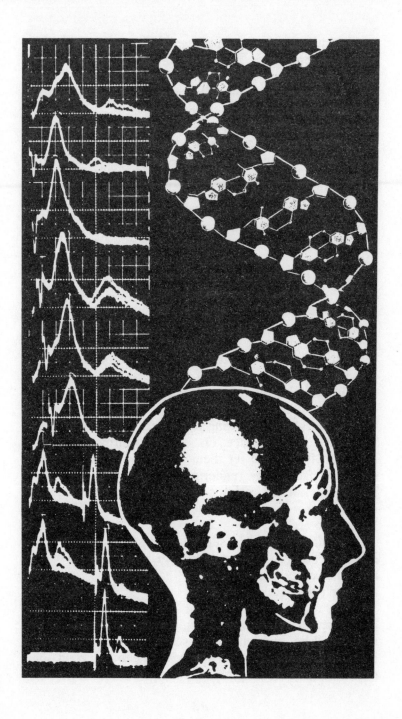

filled with books in a language you neither read nor speak, and that you've just found the dictionary and a picture reader.'

'So what are you saying? That we'll have complete understanding of how the brain operates?'

'We'll have complete *control* over how the brain operates. With chemical therapy, it will be possible to make anyone think or feel anything we want. We will have an immediate cure for all nontraumatic mental illness. We'll be able to fine-tune aggression, passion, creativity – bring them up, damp them down, it'll be all the same. You can see why our sponsors are so afraid of what our research might produce.'

'Not really, no. The world could use more sanity,' Gunther said.

'I agree. But who defines sanity? Many governments consider political dissent grounds for mental incarceration. This would open the doors of the brain, allowing it to be examined from the outside. For the first time, it would be possible to discover unexpressed rebellion. Modes of thought could be outlawed. The potential for abuse is not inconsiderable.

'Consider also the military applications. This knowledge combined with some of the new nanoweaponry might produce a berserker gas, allowing you to turn the enemy's armies upon their own populace. Or, easier, to throw them into a psychotic frenzy and let them turn on themselves. Cities could be pacified by rendering the citizenry catatonic. A secondary, internal reality could then be created, allowing the conqueror to use the masses as slave labour. The possibilities are endless.'

They digested this in silence. At last Hiro said, 'Jeeze, Krishna, if that's the open goods, what the hell kind of stuff do you have to hide?'

'I can't tell you.'

A minute later, Hiro was haring off again. At the foot of a nearby hill he found an immense boulder standing atilt on its small end. He danced about, trying to get good shots past it without catching his own footprints in them.

42

'So what's the problem?' Krishna said over his chip.

'The problem is, I can't arrange to see her. Ekatarina. I've left messages, but she won't answer them. And you know how it is in Bootstrap – it takes a real effort to avoid somebody who wants to see you. But she's managed it.'

Krishna said nothing.

'All I want to know is, just what's going on here?'

'She's avoiding you.'

'But why? I fell in love and she didn't, is that what you're telling me? I mean, is that a crock or what?'

'Without hearing her side of the story, I can't really say how she feels. But the odds are excellent she fell every bit as hard as you did. The difference is that you think it's a good idea, and she doesn't. So of course she's avoiding you. Contact would just make it more difficult for her to master her feelings for you.'

'Shit!'

An unexpected touch of wryness entered Krishna's voice. 'What do you want? A minute ago you were complaining that I think you're a machine. Now you're unhappy that Izmailova thinks she's not.'

'Hey, you guys! Come over here. I've found the perfect shot. You've got to see this.'

They turned to see Hiro waving at them from the hilltop. 'I thought you were leaving,' Gunther grumbled. 'You said you were sick of the Moon, and going away and never coming back. So how come you're upgrading your digs all of a sudden?'

'That was yesterday! Today, I'm a pioneer, a builder of worlds, a founder of dynasties!'

'This is getting tedious. What does it take to get a straight answer out of you?'

Hiro bounded high and struck a pose, arms wide and a little ridiculous. He staggered a bit on landing. 'Anya and I are getting married!'

Gunther and Krishna looked at each other, blank visor to blank visor. Forcing enthusiasm into his voice, Gunther said, 'Hey, no shit? Really! Congratu—'

A scream of static howled up from nowhere. Gunther winced and cut down the gain. 'My stupid radio is—'

One of the other two – they had moved together and he couldn't tell them apart at this distance – was pointing upward. Gunther tilted back his head, to look at the Earth. For a second he wasn't sure what he was looking for. Then he saw it: a diamond pinprick of light in the middle of the night. It was like a small, bright hole in reality, somewhere in continental Asia. 'What the hell is *that*?' he asked.

Softly, Hiro said, 'I think it's Vladivostok.'

By the time they were back over the Sinus Medii, that first light had reddened and faded away, and two more had blossomed. The news jockey at the Observatory was working overtime splicing together reports from the major news feeds into a montage of rumour and fear. The radio was full of talk about hits on Seoul and Buenos Aires. Those seemed certain. Strikes against Panama, Iraq, Denver and Cairo were disputed. A stealth missile had flown low over Hokkaido and been deflected into the Sea of Japan. The Swiss Orbitals had lost some factories to fragmentation satellites. There was no agreement as to the source aggressor, and though most suspicions trended in one direction, Tokyo denied everything.

Gunther was most impressed by the sound feed from a British video essayist, who said that it did not matter who had fired the first shot, or why. 'Who shall we blame? The Southern Alliance, Tokyo, General Kim, or possibly some Grey terrorist group that nobody has ever heard of before? In a world whose weapons were wired to hair triggers, the question is irrelevant. When the first device exploded, it activated autonomous programs which launched what is officially labelled "a measured response". Gorshov himself could not have prevented it. His tactical programs chose this week's three most likely aggressors – at least two of which were certainly innocent – and launched a response. Human beings had no say over it.

'Those three nations in turn had their own reflexive "measured responses". The results of which we are just

44

beginning to learn. Now we will pause for five days, while all concerned parties negotiate. How do we know this? Abstracts of all major defence programs are available on any public data net. They are no secret. Openness is in fact what deterrence is all about.

'We have five days to avert a war that literally nobody wants. The question is, in five days can the military and political powers seize control of their own defence programming? Will they? Given the pain and anger involved, the traditional hatreds, national chauvinism, and the natural reactions of those who number loved ones among the already dead, can those in charge overcome their own natures in time to pull back from final and total war? Our best informed guess is no. No, they cannot.

'Good night, and may God have mercy on us all.'

They flew northward in silence. Even when the broadcast cut off in midword, nobody spoke. It was the end of the world, and there was nothing they could say that did not shrink to insignificance before that fact. They simply headed home.

The land about Bootstrap was dotted with graffiti, great block letters traced out in boulders: KARL OPS – EIND-HOVEN '49 and LOUISE MCTIGHE ALBU-QUERQUE NM. An enormous eye in a pyramid. ARSENAL WORLD RUGBY CHAMPS with a crown over it. CORNPONE. Pi Lambda Phi. MOTORHEADS. A giant with a club. Coming down over them, Gunther reflected that they all referred to places and things in the world overhead, not a one of them indigenous to the Moon. What had always seemed pointless now struck him as unspeakably sad.

It was only a short walk from the hopper pad to the vacuum garage. They didn't bother to summon a jitney.

The garage seemed strangely unfamiliar to Gunther now, though he had passed through it a thousand times. It seemed to float in its own mystery, as if everything had been removed and replaced by its exact double, rendering it different and somehow unknowable. Row upon row of parked vehicles were slanted by type within painted lines. Ceiling lights strained to reach the floor, and could not.

'Boy, is this place still!' Hiro's voice seemed unnaturally loud.

It was true. In all the cavernous reaches of the garage, not a single remote or robot service unit stirred. Not so much as a pressure-leak sniffer moved.

'Must be because of the news,' Gunther muttered. He found he was not ready to speak of the war directly. To the back of the garage, five airlocks stood all in a row. Above them a warm, yellow strip of window shone in the rock. In the room beyond, he could see the overseer moving about.

Hiro waved an arm, and the small figure within leaned forward to wave back. They trudged to the nearest lock and waited.

Nothing happened.

After a few minutes, they stepped back and away from the lock to peer up through the window. The overseer was still there, moving unhurriedly. 'Hey!' Hiro shouted over open frequency. 'You up there! Are you on the job?'

The man smiled, nodded and waved again.

'Then open the goddamned door!' Hiro strode forward, and with a final, nodding wave, the overseer bent over his controls.

'Uh, Hiro,' Gunther said, 'There's something odd about—'

The door exploded open.

It slammed open so hard and fast the door was half torn off its hinges. The air within blasted out like a charge from a cannon. For a moment the garage was filled with loose tools, parts of vacuum suits and shreds of cloth. A wrench struck Gunther a glancing blow on his arm, spinning him around and knocking him to the floor.

He stared up in shock. Bits and pieces of things hung suspended for a long, surreal instant. Then, the air fled, they began to slowly shower down. He got up awkwardly, massaging his arm through the suit. 'Hiro, are you all right? Kreesh?'

'Oh my God,' Krishna said.

46

Gunther spun around. He saw Krishna crouched in the shadow of a flatbed, over something that could not possibly be Hiro, because it bent the wrong way. He walked through shimmering unreality and knelt beside Krishna. He stared down at Hiro's corpse.

Hiro had been standing directly before the door when the overseer opened it without depressurizing the corridor within first. He had caught the blast straight on. It had lifted him and smashed him against the side of the flatbed, snapping his spine and shattering his helmet visor with the backlash. He must have died instantaneously.

'Who's there?' a woman said.

A jitney had entered the garage without Gunther's noticing it. He looked up in time to see a second enter, and then a third. People began piling out. Soon there were some twenty individuals advancing across the garage. They broke into two groups. One headed straight towards the locks, and the smaller group advanced on Gunther and his friends. It looked for all the world like a military operation. 'Who's there?' the woman repeated.

Gunther lifted his friend's corpse in his arms and stood. 'It's Hiro,' he said flatly. 'Hiro.'

They floated forward cautiously, a semicircle of blank-visored suits like so many kachinas. He could make out the corporate logos. Mitsubishi. Westinghouse. Holst Orbital. Izmailova's red-and-orange suit was among them, and a vivid Mondrian pattern he didn't recognize. The woman spoke again, tensely, warily. 'Tell me how you're feeling, Hiro.'

It was Beth Hamilton.

'That's not Hiro,' Krishna said. 'It's Gunther. *That's* Hiro. That he's carrying. We were out in the highlands and . . .' His voice cracked and collapsed in confusion.

'Is that you, Krishna?' someone asked. 'There's a touch of luck. Send him up front, we're going to need him when we get in.' Somebody else slapped an arm over Krishna's shoulders and led him away.

Over the radio, a clear voice spoke to the overseer. 'Dmitri, is that you? It's Signe. You remember me, don't you, Dmitri? Signe Ohmstede. I'm your friend.'

47

'Sure I remember you, Signe. I remember you. How could I ever forget my friend? Sure I do.'

'Oh, good. I'm so happy. Listen carefully, Dmitri. Everything's fine.'

Indignantly, Gunther chinned his radio to send. 'The hell it is! That fool up there—'

A burly man in a Westinghouse suit grabbed Gunther's bad arm and shook him. 'Shut the fuck *up!*' he growled. 'This is serious, damn you. We don't have the time to baby you.'

Hamilton shoved between them. 'For God's sake, Posner, he's just seen—' She stopped. 'Let me take care of him. I'll get him calmed down. Just give us half an hour, okay?'

The others traded glances, nodded, and turned away.

To Gunther's surprise, Ekatarina spoke over his trance chip. 'I'm sorry, Gunther,' she murmured. Then she was gone.

He was still holding Hiro's corpse. He found himself staring down at his friend's ruined face. The flesh was bruised and as puffy-looking as an overboiled hot dog. He couldn't look away.

'Come on.' Beth gave him a little shove to get him going. 'Put the body in the back of that pick-up and give us a drive out to the cliff.'

At Hamilton's insistence, Gunther drove. He found it helped, having something to do. Hands afloat on the steering wheel, he stared ahead looking for the Mausoleum road cut-off. His eyes felt scratchy, and inhumanly dry.

'There was a pre-emptive strike against us,' Hamilton said. 'Sabotage. We're just now starting to put the pieces together. Nobody knew you were out on the surface or we would've sent somebody out to meet you. It's all been something of a shambles here.'

He drove on in silence, cushioned and protected by all those kilometres of hard vacuum wrapped about him. He could feel the presence of Hiro's corpse in the back of the truck, a constant psychic itch between his shoulder blades.

48

But so long as he didn't speak, he was safe; he could hold himself aloof from the universe that held the pain. It couldn't touch him. He waited, but Beth didn't add anything to what she'd already said.

Finally he said, 'Sabotage?'

'A software meltdown at the radio station. Explosions at all the railguns. Three guys from Microspacecraft Applications bought it when the Boitsovij Kot railgun blew. I suppose it was inevitable. All the military industry up here, it's not surprising somebody would want to knock us out of the equation. But that's not all. Something's happened to the people in Bootstrap. Something really horrible. I was out at the Observatory when it happened. The newsjay called back to see if there was any back-up software to get the station going again, and she got nothing but gibberish. Crazy stuff. I mean, *really* crazy. We had to disconnect the Observatory's remotes, because the operators were. . . ' She was crying now, softly and insistently, and it was a minute before she could speak again. 'Some sort of biological weapon. That's all we know.'

'We're here.'

As he pulled up to the foot of the Mausoleum cliff, it occurred to Gunther that they hadn't thought to bring a drilling rig. Then he counted ten black niches in the rockface, and realized that somebody had been thinking ahead.

'The only people who weren't hit were those who were working at the Centre or the Observatory, or out on the surface. Maybe a hundred of us all told.'

They walked around to the back of the pick-up. Gunther waited, but Hamilton didn't offer to carry the body. For some reason that made him feel angry and resentful. He unlatched the gate, hopped up on the treads, and hoisted the suited corpse. 'Let's get this over with.'

Before today, only six people had ever died on the Moon. They walked past the caves in which their bodies awaited eternity. Gunther knew their names by heart: Heisse, Yasuda, Spehalski, Dubinin, Mikami, Castillo. And now Hiro. It seemed incomprehensible that the day should ever

49

come when there would be too many dead to know them all by name.

Daisies and tiger lilies had been scattered before the vaults in such profusion that he couldn't help crushing some underfoot.

They entered the first empty niche, and he laid Hiro down upon a stone table cut into the rock. In the halo of his helmet lamp the body looked piteously twisted and uncomfortable. Gunther found that he was crying, large hot tears that crawled down his face and got into his mouth when he inhaled. He cut off the radio until he had managed to blink the tears away. 'Shit.' He wiped a hand across his helmet. 'I suppose we ought to say something.'

Hamilton took his hand and squeezed.

'I've never seen him as happy as he was today. He was going to get married. He was jumping around, laughing and talking about raising a family. And now he's dead, and I don't even know what his religion was.' A thought occurred to him, and he turned helplessly towards Hamilton. 'What are we going to tell Anya?'

'She's got problems of her own. Come on, say a prayer and let's go. You'll run out of oxygen.'

'Yeah, okay.' He bowed his head. *The Lord is my shepherd, I shall not want. . .* '

Back at Bootstrap, the surface party had seized the airlocks and led the overseer away from the controls. The man from Westinghouse, Posner, looked down on them from the observation window. 'Don't crack your suits,' he warned. 'Keep them sealed tight at all times. Whatever hit the bastards here is still around. Might be in the water, might be in the air. One whiff and you're out of here! You got that?'

'Yeah, yeah,' Gunther grumbled. 'Keep your shirt on.'

Posner's hand froze on the controls. 'Let's get serious here. I'm not letting you in until you acknowledge the gravity of the situation. This isn't a picnic outing. If you're not prepared to help, we don't need you. Is that understood?'

'We understand completely, and we'll cooperate to the fullest,' Hamilton said quickly. *'Won't we*, Weil?'

He nodded miserably.

Only the one lock had been breached, and there were five more sets of pressurized doors between it and the bulk of Bootstrap's air. The city's designers had been cautious.

Overseen by Posner, they passed through the corridors, locks and changing rooms and up the cargo escalators. Finally they emerged into the city interior.

They stood blinking on the lip of Hell.

At first, it was impossible to pinpoint any source for the pervasive sense of wrongness nattering at the edge of consciousness. The parks were dotted with people, the fill lights at the juncture of crater walls and canopy were bright, and the waterfalls still fell gracefully from terrace to terrace. Button quail bobbed comically in the grass.

Then small details intruded. A man staggered about the fourth level, head jerking, arms waving stiffly. A plump woman waddled by, pulling an empty cart made from a wheeled microfactory stand, quacking like a duck. Someone sat in the knee-high forest by Noguchi Park, tearing out the trees one by one.

But it was the still figures that were on examination more profoundly disturbing. Here a man lay half in and half out of a tunnel entrance, as unselfconscious as a dog. There, three women stood in extreme postures of lassitude, bordering on despair. Everywhere, people did not touch or speak or show in any way that they were aware of one other. They shared an absolute and universal isolation.

'What shall we—' Something slammed on to Gunther's back. He was knocked forward, off his feet. Tumbling, he became aware that fists were striking him, again and again, and then that a lean man was kneeling atop his chest, hysterically shouting, 'Don't do it! Don't do it!'

Hamilton seized the man's shoulders, and pulled him away. Gunther got to his knees. He looked into the face of madness: eyes round and fearful, expression full of panic. The man was terrified of Gunther.

With an abrupt wrench, the man broke free. He ran as if pursued by demons. Hamilton stared after him. 'You okay?' she asked.

'Yeah, sure.' Gunther adjusted his tool harness. 'Let's see if we can find the others.'

They walked towards the lake, staring about at the self-absorbed figures scattered about the grass. Nobody attempted to speak to them. A woman ran by, barefooted. Her arms were filled with flowers. 'Hey!' Hamilton called after her. She smiled fleetingly over her shoulder, but did not slow. Gunther knew her vaguely, an executive supervisor for Martin Marietta.

'Is *every*body here crazy?' he asked.

'Sure looks that way.'

The woman had reached the shore and was flinging the blossoms into the water with great sweeps of her arm. They littered the surface.

'Damned waste.' Gunther had come to Bootstrap before the flowers; he knew the effort involved getting permission to plant them and rewriting the city's ecologics. A man in a blue-striped Krupp suit was running along the verge of the lake.

The woman, flowers gone, threw herself into the water.

At first it appeared she'd suddenly decided to take a dip. But from the struggling, floundering way she thrashed deeper into the water it was clear that she could not swim.

In the time it took Gunther to realize this, Hamilton had leaped forward, running for the lake. Belatedly, he started after her. But the man in the Krupp suit was ahead of them both. He splashed in after the woman. An outstretched hand seized her shoulder and then he fell, pulling her under. She was red-faced and choking when he emerged again, arm across her chest.

By then Gunther and Beth were wading into the lake, and together they three got the woman to shore. When she was released, the woman calmly turned and walked away, as if nothing had happened.

'Gone for more flowers,' the Krupp component explained. 'This is the third time fair Ophelia there's tried to drown herself. She's not the only one. I've been hanging around, hauling 'em out when they stumble in.'

'Do you know where everybody else is? Is there anyone in charge? Somebody giving out orders?'

'Do you need any help?' Gunther asked.

The Krupp man shrugged. 'I'm fine. No idea where the others are, though. My friends were going on to the second level when I decided I ought to stay here. If you see them, you might tell 'em I'd appreciate hearing back from them. Three guys in Krupp suits.'

'We'll do that,' Gunther said.

Hamilton was already walking away.

On a step just beneath the top of the stairs sprawled one of Gunther's fellow G5 components. 'Sidney,' he said carefully. 'How's it going?'

Sidney giggled. 'I'm making the effort, if that's what you mean. I don't see that the "how" of it makes much difference.'

'Okay.'

'A better way of phrasing that might be to ask why I'm not at work.' He stood, and in a very natural manner accompanied Gunther up the steps. 'Obviously I can't be two places at once. You wouldn't want to perform major surgery in your own absence, would you?' He giggled again. 'It's an oxymoron. Like horses: those classically beautiful Praxitelesian bodies excreting these long surreal turds.'

'Okay.'

'I've always admired them for squeezing so much art into a single image.'

'Sidney,' Hamilton said. 'We're looking for our friends. Three people in blue-striped work suits.'

'I've seen them. I know just where they went.' His eyes were cool and vacant; they didn't seem to focus on anything in particular.

'Can you lead us to them?'

'Even a flower recognizes its own face.' A gracefully winding gravel path led through private garden plots and croquet malls. They followed him down it.

There were not many people on the second terrace; with the fall of madness, most seemed to have retreated into the caves. Those few who remained either ignored or cringed away from them. Gunther found himself staring obsessively into their faces, trying to analyse the deficiency he felt in each. Fear nested in their eyes – and the appalled awareness that some terrible thing had happened to them, coupled with a complete ignorance of its nature.

'God, these people!'

Hamilton grunted.

He felt he was walking through a dream. Sounds were muted by his suit, and colours less intense seen through his helmet visor. It was as if he had been subtly removed from the world, there and not-there simultaneously, an impression that strengthened with each new face that looked straight through him with mad, unseeing indifference.

Sidney turned a corner, broke into a trot and jogged into a tunnel entrance. Gunther ran after him. At the mouth of the tunnel, he paused to let his helmet adjust to the new light levels. When it cleared he saw Sidney dart down a side passage. He followed.

At the intersection of passages, he looked and saw no trace of their guide. Sidney had disappeared. 'Did you see which way he went?' he asked Hamilton over the radio. There was no answer. 'Beth?'

He started down the corridor, halted, and turned back. These things went deep. He could wander around in them for ever. He went back out to the terraces. Hamilton was nowhere to be seen.

For lack of any better plan, he followed the path. Just beyond an ornamental holly bush he was pulled up short by a vision straight out of William Blake.

The man had discarded shirt and sandals, and wore only a pair of shorts. He squatted atop a boulder, alert, patient, eating a tomato. A steel pipe slanted across his knees like a staff or sceptre, and he had woven a crown of sorts from platinum wire with a fortune's worth of hyperconductor chips dangling over his forehead. He looked every inch a kingly animal.

He stared at Gunther, calm and unblinking.

Gunther shivered. The man seemed less human than anthropoid, crafty in its way, but unthinking. He felt as if

55

he were staring across the eons at Grandfather Ape crouched on the edge of awareness. An involuntary thrill of superstitious awe seized him. Was this what happened when the higher mental functions were scraped away? Did Archetype lie just beneath the skin, waiting for the opportunity to emerge?

'I'm looking for my friend,' he said. 'A woman in a G5 suit like mine. Have you seen her? She was looking for three—' He stopped. The man was staring at him blankly. 'Oh, never mind.'

He turned away and walked on.

After a time, he lost all sense of continuity. Existence fragmented into unconnected images: a man bent almost double, leering and squeezing a yellow rubber duckie. A woman leaping up like a jack-in-the-box from behind an air monitor, shrieking and flapping her arms. An old friend sprawled on the ground, crying, with a broken leg. When he tried to help her, she scrabbled away from him in fear. He couldn't get near to her without doing more harm. 'Stay here,' he said. 'I'll find help.' Five minutes later he realized that he was lost, with not the slightest notion of how to find his way back to her again. He came to the stairs leading back down to the bottom level. There was no reason to go down them. There was no reason not to. He went down.

He had just reached the bottom of the stairs when someone in a lavender boutique suit hurried by.

Gunther chinned on his helmet radio.

'Hello!' The lavender suit glanced back at him, its visor a plate of obsidian, but did not turn back. 'Do you know where everyone's gone? I'm totally lost. How can I find out what I should be doing?' The lavender suit ducked into a tunnel.

Faintly, a voice answered, 'Try the city manager's office.'

The city manager's office was a tight little cubby an eighth of a kilometre deep within the tangled maze of administrative and service tunnels. It had never been very important in the scheme of things. The city manager's prime duties were keeping the air and water replenished and scheduling airlock inspections, functions any computer could handle better than a man had they dared trust them to a machine. The room had probably never been as crowded as it was now. Dozens of people suited for full vacuum spilled out into the hall, anxiously listening to Ekatarina confer with the city's Crisis Management Program. Gunther pushed in as close as he could; even so, he could barely see her.

'—the locks, the farms and utilities, and we've locked away all the remotes. What comes next?'

Ekatarina's peecee hung from her work harness, amplifying the CMP's silent voice. 'Now that elementary control has been established, second priority must go to the industrial sector. The factories must be locked down. The reactors must be put to sleep. There is not sufficient human supervisory presence to keep them running. The factories have mothballing programs available upon request.

'Third, the farms cannot tolerate neglect. Fifteen minutes without oxygen, and all the tilapia will die. The calimari are even more delicate. Three experienced agricultural components must be assigned immediately. Double that number if you only have inexperienced components. Advisory software is available. What are your resources?'

'Let me get back to you on that. What else?'

'What about the people?' a man asked belligerently. 'What the hell are you worrying about factories for, when our people are in the state they're in?'

Izmailova looked up sharply. 'You're one of Chang's research components, aren't you? Why are you here? Isn't there enough for you to do?' She looked about, as if abruptly awakened from sleep. 'All of you! What are you waiting for?'

'You can't put us off that easily! Who made you the little brass-plated general? We don't have to take orders from you.'

The bystanders shuffled uncomfortably, not leaving, waiting to take their cue from each other. Their suits were as good as identical in this crush, their helmets blank and expressionless. They looked like so many ambulatory eggs.

The crowd's mood balanced on the instant, ready to fall into acceptance or anger with a featherweight's push. Gunther raised an arm. 'General!' he said loudly. 'Private Weil here! I'm awaiting my orders. Tell me what to do.'

Laughter rippled through the room, and the tension eased. Ekatarina said, 'Take whoever's nearest you, and start clearing the afflicted out of the administrative areas. Guide them out towards the open, where they won't be so likely to hurt themselves. Whenever you get a room or corridor emptied, lock it up tight. Got that?'

'Yes, ma'am.' He tapped the suit nearest him, and its helmet dipped in a curt nod. But when they turned to leave their way was blocked by the crush of bodies.

'You!' Ekatarina jabbed a finger. 'Go to the farmlocks and foam them shut; I don't want any chance of getting them contaminated. Anyone with experience running factories – that's most of us, I think – should find a remote and get to work shutting the things down. The CMP will help direct you. If you have nothing else to do, buddy up and work at clearing out the corridors. I'll call a general meeting when we've put together a more comprehensive plan of action.' She paused. 'What have I left out?'

Surprisingly, the CMP answered her: 'There are twenty-three children in the city, two of them seven-year-old pre-legals and the rest five years of age or younger, offspring of registered-permanent lunar components. Standing directives are that children be given special care and protection. The third-level chapel can be converted to a care centre. Word should be spread that as they are found, the children are to be brought there. Assign one reliable individual to oversee them.'

'My God, yes.' She turned to the belligerent man from the Centre and snapped, 'Do it.'

He hesitated, then saluted ironically and turned to go.

That broke the logjam. The crowd began to disperse. Gunther and his co-worker – it turned out to be Liza Nagenda, another ground-rat like himself – set to work.

In after years Gunther was to remember this period as a

time when his life entered a dark tunnel. For long, night-marish hours he and Liza shuffled from office to storage room, struggling to move the afflicted out of the corporate areas and into the light.

The afflicted did not cooperate.

The first few rooms they entered were empty. In the fourth, a distraught-looking woman was furiously going through drawers and files and flinging their contents away. Trash covered the floor. 'It's in here somewhere, it's in here somewhere,' she said frantically.

'What's in there, darling?' Gunther said soothingly. He had to speak loudly so he could be heard through his helmet. 'What are you looking for?'

She tilted her head up with a smile of impish delight. Using both hands, she smoothed back her hair, elbows high, pushing it straight over her skull, then tucking in stray strands behind her ears. 'It doesn't matter, because I'm sure to find it now. Two scarabs appear, and between them the blazing disc of the sun; that's a good omen, not to mention being an analogy for sex. I've had sex, all the sex anyone could want, buggered behind the outhouse by the lizard king when I was nine. What did I care? I had wings then and thought that I could fly.'

Gunther edged a little closer. 'You're not making any sense at all.'

'You know, Tolstoy said there was a green stick in the woods behind his house that once found would cause all men to love one another. I believe in that green stick as a basic principle of physical existence. The universe exists in a matrix of four dimensions which we can perceive and seven which we cannot, which is why we experience peace and brotherhood as a seven-dimensional green stick phenomenon.'

'You've got to listen to me.'

'Why? You gonna tell me Hitler is dead? I don't believe in that kind of crap.'

'Oh hell,' Nagenda said. 'You can't reason with a flick. Just grab her arms and we'll chuck her out.'

It wasn't that easy, though. The woman was afraid of

them. Whenever they approached her, she slipped fearfully away. If they moved slowly, they could not corner her, and when they both rushed her, she leaped up over a desk and then down into the kneehole. Nagenda grabbed her legs and pulled. The woman wailed, and clutched at the knees of her suit. 'Get offa me,' Liza snarled. 'Gunther, get this crazy woman off my damn legs.'

'Don't kill me!' the woman screamed. 'I've always voted twice – you know I did. I told them you were a gangster, but I was wrong. Don't suck the oxygen out of my lungs!'

They got the woman out of the office, then lost her again when Gunther turned to lock the door. She went fluttering down the corridor, with Nagenda in hot pursuit. Then she dove into another office, and they had to start all over again.

It took over an hour to drive the woman from the corridors and release her into the park. The next three went quickly enough, by contrast. The one after that was difficult again, and the fifth turned out to be the first woman they had encountered, wandered back to look for her office. When they'd brought her to the open again, Liza Nagenda said, 'That's four flicks down and three thousand, eight hundred fifty-eight to go.'

'Look—' Gunther began. And then Krishna's voice sounded over his trance chip, stiffly and with exaggerated clarity. 'Everyone is to go to the central lake immediately for an organizational meeting. Repeat: Go to the lake immediately. Go to the lake now.' He was obviously speaking over a jury-rigged transmitter. The sound was bad and his voice boomed and popped on the chip.

'All right, okay, I got that,' Liza said. 'You can shut up now.'

'Please go to the lake immediately. Everyone is to go directly to the central—'

'Sheesh.'

By the time they got out to the parklands again, the open areas were thick with people. Not just the suited figures of the survivors, either. All the afflicted were emerging from the caves and corridors of Bootstrap. They walked blindly, uncertainly, towards the lake, as if newly called from the grave. The ground level was filling with people.

'Sonofabitch,' Gunther said wonderingly.

'Gunther?' Nagenda asked. 'What's going on?'

'It's the trance chips! Sonofabitch, all we had to do was speak to them over the chips. They'll do whatever the voice in their heads tells them to do.'

The land about the lake was so crowded that Gunther had trouble spotting any other suits. Then he saw a suited figure standing on the edge of the second level waving broadly. He waved back and headed for the stairs.

By the time he got to level two, a solid group of the unafflicted had gathered. More and more came up, drawn by the concentration of suits. Finally Ekatarina spoke over the open channel of her suit radio.

'There's no reason to wait for us all to gather. I think everyone is close enough to hear me. Sit down, take a little rest, you've all earned it.' People eased down on the grass. Some sprawled on their backs or stomachs, fully suited. Most just sat.

'By a fortunate accident, we've discovered a means of controlling our afflicted friends.' There was light applause. 'But there are still many problems before us, and they won't all be solved so easily. We've all seen the obvious. Now I must tell you of worse. If the war on Earth goes full thermonuclear, we will be completely and totally cut off, possibly for decades.'

A murmur passed through the crowd.

'What does this mean? Beyond the immediate inconveniences – no luxuries, no more silk shirts, no new seed stock, no new videos, no way home for those of us who hadn't already decided to stay – we will be losing much that we require for survival. All our microfacturing capability comes from the Swiss Orbitals. Our water reserves are sufficient for a year, but we lose minute quantities of water vapour to rust and corrosion and to the vacuum every time somebody goes in or out an airlock, and those quantities are necessary for our existence.

'But we can survive. We can process raw hydrogen and

61

oxygen from the regolith, and burn them to produce water. We already make our own air. We can do without most nanoelectronics. We can thrive and prosper and grow, even if Earth ... even if the worst happens. But to do so we'll need our full manufacturing capability, and full supervisory capability as well. We must not only restore our factories, but find a way to restore our people. There'll be work and more for all of us in the days ahead.'

Nagenda touched helmets with Gunther and muttered, 'What a crock.'

'Come on, I want to hear this.'

'Fortunately, the Crisis Management Program has contingency plans for exactly this situation. According to its records, which may be incomplete, I have more military command experience than any other functional. Does anyone wish to challenge this?' She waited, but nobody said anything. 'We will go to a quasimilitary structure for the duration of the emergency. This is strictly for organizational purposes. There will be no privileges afforded the officers, and the military structure will be dismantled *immediately* upon resolution of our present problems. That's paramount.'

She glanced down at her peecee. 'To that purpose, I am establishing beneath me a triumvirate of subordinate officers, consisting of Carlos Diaz-Rodrigues, Miiko Ezumi and Will Posner. Beneath them will be nine officers, each responsible for a cadre of no more than ten individuals.'

She read out names. Gunther was assigned to Cadre Four, Beth Hamilton's group. Then Ekatarina said, 'We're all tired. The gang back at the Centre have rigged up a decontamination procedure, a kitchen and sleeping spaces of sorts. Cadres One, Two and Three will put in four more hours here, then pull down a full eight hours' sleep. Cadres Four through Nine may return now to the centre for a meal and four hours' rest.' She stopped. 'That's it. Go get some shut-eye.'

A ragged cheer arose, fell flat and died. Gunther stood. Liza Nagenda gave him a friendly squeeze on the butt, and when he started to the right yanked his arm and pointed him left, towards the service escalators.

They trudged off

There was too much to do. They worked to exhaustion – it was not enough. They rigged a system of narrow-band radio transmissions for the CMP and ran a microwave patch back to the Centre, so it could direct their efforts more efficiently – it was not enough. They organized and rearranged constantly. But the load was too great and accients inevitably happened.

Half the surviving railguns – small units to deliver raw and semiprocessed materials over the highlands and across the bay – were badly damaged when the noonday sun buckled their aluminium rails; the sunscreens had not been put in place in time. An unknown number of robot bull-dozers had wandered off from the strip mines and were presumably lost. It was hard to guess how many because the inventory records were scrambled. None of the food stored in Bootstrap could be trusted; the Centre's meals had to be harvested direct from the farms and taken out through the emergency locks. An inexperienced farmer mis-handled her remote, and ten aquaculture tanks boiled out into vacuum, geysering nine thousand fingerlings across the surface. On Posner's orders, the remote handler rigs were hastily packed and moved to the Centre. When uncrated, most were found to have damaged rocker arms.

There were small victories. On his second shift, Gunther found fourteen bales of cotton in vacuum storage and set an assembler to sewing futons for the Centre. That meant an end to sleeping on bare floors and made him a local hero for the rest of that day. There were not enough toilets in the Centre; Diaz-Rodrigues ordered the flare storm shelters in the factories stripped of theirs. Huriel Garza dis-covered a talent for cooking with limited resources.

But they were losing ground. The afflicted were unpre-dictable, and they were everywhere. A demented systems analyst, obeying the voices in his head, dumped several barrels of lubricating oil in the lake. The water filters clogged, and the streams had to be shut down for repairs. A doctor somehow managed to strangle herself with her own diagnostic harness. The city's ecologics were badly stressed by random vandalism.

Finally somebody thought to rig up a voice loop for continuous transmission. 'I am calm,' it said. 'I am tranquil. I do not want to do anything. I am happy where I am.'

Gunther was working with Liza Nagenda, trying to get the streams going again, when the loop came on. He looked up and saw an uncanny quiet spread over Bootstrap. Up and down the terraces, the flicks stood in postures of complete and utter impassivity. The only movement came from the small number of suits scurrying like beetles among the newly catatonic.

Liza put her hands on her hips. 'Terrific. Now we've got to *feed* them.'

She was right. Relieved as he was, Gunther knew it. One hopeless task had been traded for another.

He was wearily suiting up for his third day when Hamilton stopped him and said, 'Weil! You know any electrical engineering?'

'Not really, no. I mean, I can do the wiring for a truck, or maybe rig up a microwave relay, stuff like that, but . . .'

'It'll have to do. Drop what you're on, and help Krishna set up a system for controlling the flicks. Some way we can handle them individually.'

They set up shop in Krishna's old lab. The remnants of old security standards still lingered, and nobody had been allowed to sleep there. Consequently, the room was wonderfully neat and clean, all crafted-in-orbit laboratory equipment with smooth, anonymous surfaces. It was a throwback to a time before clutter and madness had taken over. If it weren't for the new-tunnel smell, the raw tang of cut rock the air carried, it would be possible to pretend nothing had happened.

Gunther stood in a telepresence rig, directing a remote through Bootstrap's apartments. They were like so many unconnected cells of chaos. He entered one and found the words BUDDHA = COSMIC INERTIA scrawled on its wall with what looked to be human faeces. A woman sat on the futon tearing handfuls of batting from it and flinging them in the air. Cotton covered the room like a fresh snowfall. The next apartment was empty and clean, and a microfactory sat gleaming on a ledge. 'I hereby nationalize you in the name of the People's Provisional Republic of Bootstrap, and of the oppressed masses everywhere,' he said dryly. The remote gingerly picked it up. 'You done with that chip diagram yet?'

'It will not be long now,' Krishna said.

They were building a prototype controller. The idea was to code each peecee, so the CMP could identify and speak to its owner individually. By stepping down the voltage, they could limit the peecee's transmission range to a metre and a half so that each afflicted person could be given individualized orders. The existing chips, however, were high-strung Swiss Orbital thoroughbreds, and couldn't handle oddball power yields. They had to be replaced.

'I don't see how you can expect to get any useful work out of these guys, though. I mean, what we need are supervisors. You can't hope to get coherent thought out of them.'

Bent low over his peecee, Krishna did not answer at first. Then he said, 'Do you know how a yogi stops his heart? We looked into that when I was in grad school. We asked Yogi Premanand if he would stop his heart while wired up to our instruments, and he graciously consented. We had all the latest brain scanners, but it turned out the most interesting results were recorded by the EKG.

'We found that the yogi's heart did not as we had expected slow down, but rather went faster and faster, until it reached its physical limits and began to fibrillate. He had not slowed his heart; he had sped it up. It did not stop, but went into spasm.

'After our tests, I asked him if he had known these facts. He said no, that they were most interesting. He was polite about it, but clearly did not think our findings very significant.'

'So you're saying . . .?'

'The problem with schizophrenics is that they have too much going on in their heads. Too many voices. Too many ideas. They can't focus their attention on a single chain of thought. But it would be a mistake to think them incapable of complex reasoning. In fact, they're thinking brilliantly. Their brains are simply operating at such peak efficiencies that they can't organize their thoughts coherently.

'What the trance chip does is to provide one more voice, but a louder, more insistent one. That's why they obey it. It breaks through that noise, provides a focus, serves as a matrix along which thought can crystallize.'

The remote unlocked the door into a conference room deep in the administrative tunnels. Eight microfactories waited in a neat row atop the conference table. It added the ninth, turned, and left, locking the door behind it. 'You know,' Gunther said, 'all these elaborate precautions may be unnecessary. Whatever was used on Bootstrap may not be in the air any more. It may never have *been* in the air. It could've been in the water or something.'

'Oh, it's there all right, in the millions. We're dealing with an airborne schizomimetic engine. It's designed to hang around in the air indefinitely.'

'A schizomimetic engine? What the hell is that?'

In a distracted monotone, Krishna said, 'A schizomimetic engine is a strategic nonlethal weapon with high psychological impact. It not only incapacitates its target vectors, but places a disproportionately heavy burden on the enemy's manpower and material support caring for the victims. Due to the particular quality of the effect, it has a profoundly demoralizing influence on those exposed to the victims, especially those involved in their care. Thus, it is particularly desirable as a strategic weapon.' He might have been quoting from an operations manual.

Gunther pondered that. 'Calling the meeting over the chips wasn't a mistake, was it? You knew it would work. You knew they would obey a voice speaking inside their heads.'

'Yes.'

'This shit was brewed up at the Centre, wasn't it? This is the stuff that you couldn't talk about.'

'Some of it.'

Gunther powered down his rig and flipped up the lens. 'God damn you, Krishna! God damn you straight to Hell, you stupid fucker!'

Krishna looked up from his work, bewildered. 'Have I said something wrong?'

'No! No, you haven't said a damned thing wrong – you've just driven four thousand people out of their fucking minds, is all! Wake up and take a good look at what you maniacs have done with your weapons research!'

'It wasn't weapons research,' Krishna said mildly. He drew a long, involuted line on the schematic. 'But when pure research is funded by the military, the military will seek out military applications for the research. That's just the way it is.'

'What's the difference? It happened. You're responsible.'

Now Krishna actually set his peecee aside. He spoke with uncharacteristic fire. 'Gunther, we *need* this information. Do you realize that we are trying to run a technological civilization with a brain that was evolved in the neolithic? I am perfectly serious. We're all trapped in the old hunter-gatherer programs, and they are of no use to us any more. Take a look at what's happening on Earth. They're hip-deep in a war that nobody meant to start and nobody wants to fight and it's even money that nobody can stop. The type of thinking that put us in this corner is not to our benefit. It has to change. And that's what we are working towards – taming the human brain. Harnessing it. Reining it in.

'Granted, our research has been turned against us. But what's one more weapon among so many? If neuroprogrammers hadn't been available, something else would have been used. Mustard gas maybe, or plutonium dust. For that matter, they could've just blown a hole in the canopy and let us all strangle.'

'That's self-justifying bullshit, Krishna! Nothing can excuse what you've done.'

Quietly, but with conviction, Krishna said, 'You will never convince me that our research is not the most important work we could possibly be doing today. We must seize control of this monster within our skulls. We must change our ways of thinking.' His voice dropped. 'The sad thing is that we cannot change unless we survive. But in order to survive, we must first change.'

They worked in silence after that.

Gunther awoke from restless dreams to find that the sleep shift was only half over. Liza was snoring. Careful not to wake her, he pulled his clothes on and padded barefoot out of his niche and down the hall. The light was on in the common room and he heard voices.

Ekatarina looked up when he entered. Her face was pale and drawn. Faint circles had formed under her eyes. She was alone.

'Oh, hi. I was just talking with the CMP.' She thought off her peecee. 'Have a seat.'

He pulled up a chair and hunched down over the table. Confronted by her, he found it took a slight but noticeable effort to draw his breath. 'So. How are things going?'

'They'll be trying out your controllers soon. The first batch of chips ought to be coming out of the factories in an hour or so. I thought I'd stay up to see how they work out.'

'It's that bad, then?' Ekatarina shook her head, would not look at him. 'Hey, come on, here you are waiting up on the results, and I can see how tired you are. There must be a lot riding on this thing.'

'More than you know,' she said bleakly. 'I've just been going over the numbers. Things are worse than you can imagine.'

He reached out and took her cold, bloodless hand. She squeezed him so tightly it hurt. Their eyes met and he saw in hers all the fear and wonder he felt.

Wordlessly, they stood.

'I'm niching alone,' Ekatarina said. She had not let go of his hand, held it so tightly, in fact, that it seemed she would never let it go.

Gunther let her lead him away.

They made love, and talked quietly about inconsequential

68

things, and made love again. Gunther had thought she would nod off immediately after the first time, but she was too full of nervous energy for that.

'Tell me when you're about to come,' she murmured. 'Tell me when you're coming.'

He stopped moving. 'Why do you always say that?'

Ekatarina looked up at him dazedly, and he repeated the question. Then she laughed a deep, throaty laugh. 'Because I'm frigid.'

'Hah?'

She took his hand and brushed her cheek against it. Then she ducked her head, continuing the motion across her neck and up the side of her scalp. He felt the short, prickly hair against his palm and then, behind her ear, two bumps under the skin where biochips had been implanted. One of those would be her trance chip and the other ...

'It's a prosthetic,' she explained. Her eyes were grey and solemn. 'It hooks into the pleasure centres. When I need to, I can turn on my orgasm at a thought. That way we can always come at the same time.' She moved her hips slowly beneath him as she spoke.

'But that means you don't really need to have any kind of sexual stimulation at all, do you? You can trigger an orgasm at will. While you're riding on a bus. Or behind a desk. You could just turn that thing on and come for hours at a time.'

She looked amused. 'I'll tell you a secret. When it was new, I used to do stunts like that. Everybody does. One outgrows that sort of thing quickly.'

With more than a touch of stung pride, Gunther said, 'Then what am I doing here? If you've got that thing, what the hell do you need me for?' He started to draw away from her.

She pulled him down atop her again. 'You're kind of comforting,' she said. 'In an argumentative way. Come here.'

He got back to his futon and began gathering up the pieces

of his suit. Liza sat up sleepily and gawked at him. 'So,' she said. 'It's like that, is it?'

'Yeah, well. I kind of left something unfinished. An old relationship.' Warily, he extended a hand. 'No hard feelings, huh?'

Ignoring his hand, she stood, naked and angry. 'You got the nerve to stand there without even wiping my smile off your dick first and say no hard feelings? Asshole!'

'Aw, come on now, Liza, it's not like that.'

'Like hell it's not! You got a shot at that white-assed Russian ice queen, and I'm history. Don't think I don't know all about her.'

'I was hoping we could still be, you know, friends.'

'Nice trick, shithead.' She balled her fist and hit him hard in the centre of his chest. Tears began to form in her eyes. 'You just slink away. I'm tired of looking at you.'

He left.

But did not sleep. Ekatarina was awake and ebullient over the first reports coming in of the new controller system. 'They're working!' she cried. 'They're working!' She'd pulled on a silk camisole, and strode back and forth excitedly, naked to the waist. Her pubic hair was a white flame, with almost invisible trails of smaller hairs reaching for her navel and caressing the sweet insides of her thighs. Tired as he was, Gunther felt new desire for her. In a weary, washed-out way, he was happy.

'Whooh!' She kissed him hard, not sexually, and called up the CMP. 'Rerun all our earlier projections. We're putting our afflicted components back to work,' she thought. 'Adjust all work schedules.'

'As you direct.'

'How does this change our long-range prospects?'

The program was silent for several seconds, processing. Then it said, 'You are about to enter a necessary but very dangerous stage of recovery. You are going from a low-prospects high-stability situation to a high-prospects high-instability one. With leisure your unafflicted components will quickly grow dissatisfied with your government.'

70

'What happens if I just step down?'

'Prospects worsen drastically.'

Ekatarina ducked her head. 'All right, what's likely to be our most pressing new problem?'

'The unafflicted components will demand to know more about the war on Earth. They'll want the media feeds restored immediately.'

'I could rig up a receiver easily enough,' Gunther volunteered. 'Nothing fancy, but . . .'

'Don't you dare!'

'Hah? Why not?'

'Gunther, let me put it to you this way: What two nationalities are most heavily represented here?'

'Well, I guess that would be Russia and – oh.'

'Oh is right. For the time being, I think it's best if nobody knows for sure who's supposed to be enemies with whom.' To the CMP she thought, 'How should I respond?'

'Until the situation stabilizes, you have no choice but distraction. Keep their minds occupied. Hunt down the saboteurs and then organize war crime trials.'

'That's out. No witch hunts, no scapegoats, no trials. We're all in this together.'

Emotionlessly, the CMP said, 'Violence is the left hand of government. You are rash to dismiss its potentials without serious thought.'

'I won't discuss it.'

'Very well. If you wish to postpone the use of force for the present, you could hold a hunt for the weapon used on Bootstrap. Locating and identifying it would involve everyone's energies without necessarily implicating anybody. It would also be widely interpreted as meaning an eventual cure was possible, thus boosting the general morale without your actually lying.'

Tiredly, as if this were something she had gone over many times already, she said, 'Is there really no hope of curing them?'

'Anything is possible. In light of present resources, though, it cannot be considered likely.'

71

Ekatarina thought the peecee off, dismissing the CMP. She sighed. 'Maybe that's what we ought to do. Donkey up a hunt for the weapon. We ought to be able to do something with that notion.'

Puzzled, Gunther said, 'But it was one of Chang's weapons, wasn't it? A schizomimetic engine, right?'

'Where did you hear that?' she demanded sharply.

'Well, Krishna said . . . He didn't act like . . . I thought it was public knowledge.'

Ekatarina's face hardened. 'Program!' she thought.

The CMP came back to life. 'Ready.'

'Locate Krishna Narasimhan, unafflicted, Cadre Five. I want to speak with him immediately.' Ekatarina snatched up her panties and shorts, and furiously began dressing. 'Where are my damned sandals? Program! Tell him to meet me in the common room. Right away.'

'Received.'

To Gunther's surprise, it took over an hour for Ekatarina to browbeat Krishna into submission. Finally, though, the young research component went to a lockbox, identified himself to it, and unsealed the storage areas. 'It's not all that secure,' he said apologetically. 'If our sponsors knew how often we just left everything open so we could get in and out, they'd – well, never mind.'

He lifted a flat, palm-sized metal rectangle from a cabinet. 'This is the most likely means of delivery. It's an aerosol bomb. The biological agents are loaded *here*, and it's triggered by snapping this back *here*. It's got enough pressure in it to spew the agents fifteen metres straight up. Air currents do the rest.' He tossed it to Gunther, who stared down at the thing in horror. 'Don't worry, it's not armed.'

He slid out a drawer holding row upon gleaming row of slim chrome cylinders. 'These contain the engines themselves. They're off-the-shelf nanoweaponry. State-of-the-art stuff, I guess.' He ran a fingertip over them. 'We've programmed each to produce a different mix of neurotransmitters. Dopamine, phencyclidine, norepinephrine, acetylcholine, met-enkephalin, substance P, serotonin –

72

there's a hefty slice of Heaven in here, and' – he tapped an empty space – 'right here is our missing bit of Hell.' He frowned, and muttered, 'That's curious. Why are there *two* cylinders missing?'

'What's that?' Ekatarina said. 'I didn't catch what you just said.'

'Oh, nothing important. Um, listen, it might help if I yanked a few biological pathways charts and showed you the chemical underpinnings of these things.'

'Never mind that. Just keep it sweet and simple. Tell us about these schizomimetic engines.'

It took over an hour to explain.

The engines were molecule-sized chemical factories, much like the assemblers in a microfactory. They had been provided by the military, in the hope Chang's group would come up with a misting weapon that could be sprayed in an army's path to cause them to change their loyalty. Gunther dozed off briefly while Krishna was explaining why that was impossible, and woke up some time after the tiny engines had made their way into the brain.

'It's really a false schizophrenia,' Krishna explained. 'True schizophrenia is a beautifully complicated mechanism. What these engines create is more like a bargain-basement knock-off. They seize control of the brain chemistry, and start pumping out dopamine and a few other neuro-mediators. It's not an actual disorder, *per se*. They just keep the brain hopping.' He coughed. 'You see.'

'Okay,' Ekatarina said. 'Okay. You say you can reprogram these things. How?'

'We use what are technically called messenger engines. They're like neuromodulators – they tell the schizomimetic engines what to do.' He slid open another drawer, and in a flat voice said, 'They're gone.'

'Let's keep to the topic, if we may. We'll worry about your inventory later. Tell us about these messenger engines. Can you brew up a lot of them, to tell the schizomimetics to turn themselves off?'

'No, for two reasons. First, these molecules were hand-crafted in the Swiss Orbitals; we don't have the industrial plant to create them. Secondly, you can't tell the schizo-mimetics to turn themselves off. They don't *have* off switches. They're more like catalysts than actual machines. You can reconfigure them to produce different chemicals, but ...' He stopped, and a distant look came into his eyes. 'Damn.' He grabbed up his peecee, and a chemical pathways chart appeared on one wall. Then beside it, a listing of major neurofunctions. Then another chart covered with scrawled behavioural symbols. More and more data slammed up on the wall.

'Uh, Krishna . . .?'

'Oh, go away,' he snapped. 'This is important.'

'You think you might be able to come up with a cure?'

'Cure? No. Something better. Much better.'

Ekatarina and Gunther looked at each other. Then she said, 'Do you need anything? Can I assign anyone to help you?'

'I need the messenger engines. Find them for me.'

'How? How do we find them? Where do we look?'

'Sally Chang,' Krishna said impatiently. 'She must have them. Nobody else had access.' He snatched up a light pen, and began scrawling crabbed formulae on the wall.

'I'll get her for you. Program! Tell—'

'Chang's a flick,' Gunther reminded her. 'She was caught by the aerosol bomb.' Which she must surely have set herself. A neat way of disposing of evidence that might've led to whatever government was running her. She'd have been the first to go mad.

Ekatarina pinched her nose, wincing. 'I've been awake too long,' she said. 'All right, I understand. Krishna, from now on you're assigned permanently to research. The CMP will notify your cadre leader. Let me know if you need any support. Find me a way to turn this damned weapon off.' Ignoring the way he shrugged her off, she said to Gunther, 'I'm yanking you from Cadre Four. From now on, you report directly to me. I want you to find Chang. Find her, and find those messenger engines.'

Gunther was bone-weary. He couldn't remember when

he'd last had a good eight hours' sleep. But he managed what he hoped was a confident grin. 'Received.'

A madwoman should not have been able to hide herself. Sally Chang could. Nobody should have been able to evade the CMP's notice, now that it was hooked into a growing number of afflicted individuals. Sally Chang did. The CMP informed Gunther that none of the flicks were aware of Chang's whereabouts. It accepted a directive to have them all glance about for her once every hour until she was found.

In the west tunnels, walls had been torn out to create a space as large as any factory interior. The remotes had been returned, and were now manned by almost two hundred flicks spaced so that they did not impinge upon each other's fields of instruction. Gunther walked by them, through the CMP's whispering voices: 'Are all bulldozers accounted for? If so . . . Clear away any malfunctioning machines; they can be placed . . . for vacuum-welded dust on the upper surfaces of the rails . . . reduction temperature, then look to see that the oxygen feed is compatible . . .' At the far end a single suit sat in a chair, overseer unit in its lap.

'How's it going?' Gunther asked.

'Absolutely top-notch.' He recognized Takayuni's voice. 'Most of the factories are up and running, and we're well on our way to having the railguns operative too. You wouldn't believe the kind of efficiencies we're getting here.'

'Good, huh?'

Takayuni grinned; Gunther could hear it in his voice. 'Industrious little buggers!'

Takayuni hadn't seen Chang. Gunther moved on.

Some hours later he found himself sitting wearily in Noguchi Park, looking at the torn-up dirt where the knee-high forest had been. Not a seedling had been spared; the silver birch was extinct as a lunar species. Dead carp floated belly-up in the oil-slicked central lake; a chain-link fence circled it now, to keep out the flicks. There hadn't been the time yet to begin cleaning up the litter, and when he looked about, he saw trash everywhere. It was sad. It reminded him of Earth.

He knew it was time to get going, but he couldn't. His head sagged, touched his chest, and jerked up. Time had passed.

A flicker of motion made him turn. Somebody in a pastel lavender boutique suit hurried by. The woman who had directed him to the city controller's office the other day. 'Hello!' he called. 'I found everybody just where you said. Thanks. I was starting to get a little spooked.'

The lavender suit turned to look at him. Sunlight glinted on black glass. A still, long minute later, she said, 'Don't mention it,' and started away.

'I'm looking for Sally Chang. Do you know her? Have you seen her? She's a flick, kind of a little woman, flamboyant, used to favour bright clothes, electric make-up, that sort of thing.'

'I'm afraid I can't help you.' Lavender was carrying three oxytanks in her arms. 'You might try the straw market, though. Lots of bright clothes there.' She ducked into a tunnel opening and disappeared within.

Gunther started after her distractedly, then shook his head. He felt so very, very tired.

The straw market looked as though it had been through a storm. The tents had been torn down, the stands knocked over, the goods looted. Shards of orange and green glass crunched underfoot. Yet a rack of Italian scarves worth a year's salary stood untouched amid the rubble. It made no sense at all.

Up and down the market, flicks were industriously cleaning up. They stooped and lifted and swept. One of them was being beaten by a suit.

Gunther blinked. He could not react to it as a real event. The woman cringed under the blows, shrieking wildly and scuttling away from them. One of the tents had been re-erected, and within the shadow of its rainbow silks, four other suits lounged against the bar. Not a one of them moved to help the woman.

'Hey!' Gunther shouted. He felt hideously self-conscious, as if he'd been abruptly thrust into the middle of a play without memorized lines or any idea of the plot or notion of what his role in it was. 'Stop that!'

The suit turned towards him. It held the woman's slim arm captive in one gloved hand. 'Go away,' a male voice growled over the radio.

'What do you think you're doing? Who are you?' The man wore a Westinghouse suit, one of a dozen or so among the unafflicted. But Gunther recognized a brown, kidney-shaped scorch mark on the abdomen panel. 'Posner – is that you? Let that woman go.'

'She's not a woman,' Posner said. 'Hell, look at her – she's not even human. She's a flick.'

Gunther set his helmet to record. 'I'm taping this,' he warned. 'You hit that woman again, and Ekatarina will see it all. I promise.'

Posner released the woman. She stood dazed for a second or two, and then the voice from her peecee reasserted control. She bent to pick up a broom, and returned to work.

Switching off his helmet, Gunther said, 'Okay. What did she do?'

Indignantly, Posner extended a foot. He pointed sternly down at it. 'She peed all over my boot!'

The suits in the tent had been watching with interest. Now they roared. 'Your own fault, Will!' one of them called out. 'I told you you weren't scheduling in enough time for personal hygiene.'

'Don't worry about a little moisture. It'll boil off next time you hit vacuum!'

But Gunther was not listening. He stared at the flick Posner had been mistreating and wondered why he hadn't recognized Anya earlier. Her mouth was pursed, her face squinched up tight with worry, as if there were a key in the back of her head that had been wound three times too many. Her shoulders cringed forward now, too. But still.

'I'm sorry, Anya,' he said. 'Hiro is dead. There wasn't anything we could do.'

She went on sweeping, oblivious, unhappy.

*

He caught the shift's last jitney back to the Centre. It felt good to be home again. Miiko Ezumi had decided to loot the outlying factories of their oxygen and water surpluses, then carved a shower room from the rock. There was a long line for only three minutes' use, and no soap, but nobody complained. Some people pooled their time, showering two and three together. Those waiting their turns joked rowdily.

Gunther washed, grabbed some clean shorts and a Glavkosmos tee shirt, and padded down the hall. He hesitated outside the common room, listening to the gang sitting around the table discussing the more colourful flicks they'd encountered.

'Have you seen the Mouse Hunter?'

'Oh yeah, and Ophelia!'

'The Pope!'

'The Duck Lady!'

'Everybody knows the Duck Lady!'

They were laughing and happy. A warm sense of community flowed from the room, what Gunther's father would have in his sloppy-sentimental way called *Gemütlichkeit*. Gunther stepped within.

Liza Nagenda looked up, all gums and teeth, and froze. Her jaw snapped shut. 'Well, if it isn't Izmailova's personal spy!'

'What?' The accusation took Gunther's breath away. He looked helplessly about the room. Nobody would meet his eye. They had all fallen silent.

Liza's face was grey with anger. 'You heard me! It was you that ratted on Krishna, wasn't it?'

'Now that's way out of line! You've got a lot of fucking gall if—' He controlled himself with an effort. There was no sense in matching her hysteria with his own. 'It's none of your business what my relationship with Izmailova is or is not.' He looked around the table. 'Not that any of you deserve to know, but Krishna's working on a cure. If anything I said or did helped put him back in the lab, well then, so be it.'

She smirked. 'So what's your excuse for snitching on Will Posner?'

'I never—'

'We all heard the story! You told him you were going to run straight to your precious Izmailova with your little helmet vids.'

'Now, Liza,' Takayuni began. She slapped him away.

'Do you know what Posner was doing?' Gunther shook a finger in Liza's face. 'Hah? Do you? He was beating a woman – Anya! He was beating Anya right out in the open!'

'So what? He's one of us, isn't he? Not a zoned-out, dead-eyed ranting, drooling *flick*!'

'You bitch!' Outraged, Gunther lunged at Liza across the table. 'I'll kill you, I swear it!' People jerked back from him, rushed forward, a chaos of motion. Posner thrust himself in Gunther's way, arms spread, jaw set and manly. Gunther punched him in the face. Posner looked surprised, and fell back. Gunther's hand stung, but he felt strangely good anyway; if everyone else was crazy, then why not him?

'You just try it!' Liza shrieked. 'I knew you were that type all along!'

Takayuni grabbed Liza away one way. Hamilton seized Gunther and yanked him the other. Two of Posner's friends were holding him back as well.

'I've had about all I can take from you!' Gunther shouted. 'You cheap cunt!'

'Listen to him! Listen what he calls me!'

Screaming, they were shoved out opposing doors.

'It's all right, Gunther.' Beth had flung him into the first niche they'd come to. He slumped against a wall, shaking, and closed his eyes. 'It's all right now.'

But it wasn't. Gunther was suddenly struck with the realization that with the exception of Ekatarina he no longer had any friends. Not real friends, close friends. How could this have happened? It was as if everyone had been turned into werewolves. Those who weren't actually mad were still monsters. 'I don't understand.'

Hamilton sighed. 'What don't you understand, Weil?'

'The way people – the way we all treat the flicks. When Posner was beating Anya, there were four other suits standing nearby, and not a one of them so much as lifted a finger to stop him. Not one! And I felt it too, there's no use pretending I'm superior to the rest of them. I wanted to walk on and pretend I hadn't seen a thing. What's happened to us?'

Hamilton shrugged. Her hair was short and dark about her plain round face. 'I went to a pretty expensive school when I was a kid. One year we had one of those exercises that're supposed to be personally enriching. You know? A life experience. We were divided into two groups – Prisoners and Guards. The Prisoners couldn't leave their assigned areas without permission from a guard, the Guards got better lunches, stuff like that. Very simple set of rules. I was a Guard.

'Almost immediately, we started to bully the Prisoners. We pushed 'em around, yelled at 'em, kept 'em in line. What was amazing was that the Prisoners let us do it. They outnumbered us five to one. We didn't even have authority for the things we did. But not a one of them complained. Not a one of them stood up and said No, you can't do this. They played the game.

'At the end of the month, the project was dismantled and we had some study seminars on what we'd learned: the roots of fascism, and so on. Read some Hannah Arendt. And then it was all over. Except that my best girlfriend never spoke to me again. I couldn't blame her either. Not after what I'd done.

'What did I really learn? That people will play whatever role you put them in. They'll do it without knowing that that's what they're doing. Take a minority, tell them they're special, and make them guards – they'll start playing Guard.'

'So what's the answer? How do we keep from getting caught up in the roles we play?'

'Damned if I know, Weil. Damned if I know.'

Ekatarina had moved her niche to the far end of a new tunnel. Hers was the only room the tunnel served, and consequently she had a lot of privacy. As Gunther stepped in, a staticky voice swam into focus on his trance chip. '... reported shock. In Cairo, government officials pledged ... It cut off.

'Hey! You've restored—' He stopped. If radio reception had been restored, he'd have known. It would have been the talk of the Centre. Which meant that radio contact had never really been completely broken. It was simply being controlled by the CMP.

Ekatarina looked up at him. She'd been crying, but she'd stopped. 'The Swiss Orbitals are gone!' she whispered. 'They hit them with everything from softbombs to brilliant pebbles. They dusted the shipyards.'

The scope of all those deaths obscured what she was saying for a second. He sank down beside her. 'But that means . . .'

'There's no spacecraft that can reach us, yes. Unless there's a ship in transit, we're stranded here.'

He took her in his arms. She was cold and shivering. Her skin felt clammy and mottled with gooseflesh. 'How long has it been since you've had any sleep?' he asked sharply.

'I can't—'

'You're wired, aren't you?'

'I can't afford to sleep. Not now. Later.'

'Ekatarina. The energy you get from wire isn't free. It's only borrowed from your body. When you come down, it all comes due. If you wire yourself up too tightly, you'll crash yourself right into a coma.'

'I haven't been—' She stalled, and a confused, uncertain look entered her eyes. 'Maybe you're right. I could probably use a little rest.'

The CMP came to life. 'Cadre Nine is building a radio receiver. Ezumi gave them the go-ahead.'

'Shit!' Ekatarina sat bolt upright. 'Can we stop it?'

'Moving against a universally popular project would cost you credibility you cannot afford to lose.'

'Okay, so how can we minimize the—'

'Ekatarina,' Gunther said. 'Sleep, remember?'

'In a sec, babe.' She patted the futon. 'You just lie down and wait for me. I'll have this wrapped up before you can nod off.' She kissed him gently, lingeringly. 'All right?'

'Yeah, sure.' He lay down and closed his eyes, just for a second.

When he awoke, it was time to go on shift, and Ekatarina was gone.

It was only the fifth day since Vladivostok. But everything was so utterly changed that times before then seemed like memories of another world. In a previous life I was Gunther Weil, he thought. I lived and worked and had a few laughs. Life was pretty good then.

He was still looking for Sally Chang, though with dwindling hope. Now, whenever he talked to suits he'd ask if they needed his help. Increasingly, they did not.

The third-level chapel was a shallow bowl facing the terrace wall. Tiger lilies grew about the chancel area at the bottom, and turquoise lizards skittered over the rock. The children were playing with a ball in the chancel. Gunther stood at the top, chatting with a sad-voiced Ryohei Iomato.

The children put away the ball and began to dance. They were playing London Bridge. Gunther watched them with a smile. From above they were so many spots of colour, a flower unfolding and closing in on itself. Slowly, the smile faded. They were dancing too well. Not one of the children moved out of step, lost her place, or walked away sulking. Their expressions were intense, self-absorbed, inhuman. Gunther had to turn away.

'The CMP controls them,' Iomato said. 'I don't have much to do, really. I go through the vids and pick out games for them to play, songs to sing, little exercises to keep them healthy. Sometimes I have them draw.'

'My God, how can you stand it?'

Iomato sighed. 'My old man was an alcoholic. He had a pretty rough life, and at some point he started drinking to blot out the pain. You know what?'

'It didn't work.'

'Yah. Made him even more miserable. So then he had

twice the reason to get drunk. He kept on trying, though, I've got to give him that. He wasn't the sort of man to give up on something he believed in just because it wasn't working the way it should.'

Gunther said nothing.

'I think that memory is the only thing keeping me from taking off my helmet and joining them.'

The Corporate Video Centre was a narrow run of offices in the farthest tunnel reaches, where raw footage for adverts and incidental business use was processed before being squirted to better-equipped vid centres on Earth. Gunther passed from office to office, slapping off flatscreens left flickering since the disaster.

It was unnerving going through the normally busy rooms and finding no one. The desks and cluttered work stations had been abandoned in purposeful disarray, as though their operators had merely stepped out for a break and would be back momentarily. Gunther found himself spinning around to confront his shadow, and flinching at unexpected noises. With each machine he turned off, the silence at his back grew. It was twice as lonely as being out on the surface.

He doused a last light and stepped into the gloomy hall. Two suits with interwoven H-and-A logos loomed up out of the shadows. He jumped in shock. The suits did not move. He laughed wryly at himself, and pushed past. They were empty, of course – there were no Hyundai Aerospace components among the unafflicted. Someone had simply left these suits here in temporary storage before the madness.

The suits grabbed him.

'Hey!' He shouted in terror as they seized him by the arms and lifted him off his feet. One of them hooked the peecee from his harness and snapped it off. Before he knew what was happening he'd been swept down a short flight of stairs and through a doorway.

'Mr Weil.'

He was in a high-ceilinged room carved into the rock to hold air-handling equipment that hadn't been constructed

83

yet. A high string of temporary work lamps provided dim light. To the far side of the room a suit sat behind a desk, flanked by two or more, standing. They all wore Hyundai Aerospace suits. There was no way he could identify them.

The suits that had brought him in crossed their arms.

'What's going on here?' Gunther asked. 'Who are you?'

'You are the last person we'd tell that to.' He couldn't tell which one had spoken. The voice came over his radio, made sexless and impersonal by an electronic filter. 'Mr Weil, you stand accused of crimes against your fellow citizens. Do you have anything to say in your defence.'

'What?' Gunther looked at the suits before him and to either side. They were perfectly identical, indistinguishable from each other, and he was suddenly afraid of what the people within might feel free to do, armoured as they were in anonymity. 'Listen, you've got no right to do this. There's a governmental structure in place, if you've got any complaints against me.'

'Not everyone is pleased with Izmailova's government,' the judge said.

'But she controls the CMP, and we could not run Bootstrap without the CMP controlling the flicks,' a second added.

'We simply have to work around her.' Perhaps it was the judge; perhaps it was yet another of the suits. Gunther couldn't tell.

'Do you wish to speak on your own behalf?'

'What exactly am I charged with?' Gunther asked desperately. 'Okay, maybe I've done something wrong; I'll entertain that possibility. But maybe you just don't understand my situation. Have you considered that?'

Silence.

'I mean, just what are you angry about? Is it Posner? Because I'm not sorry about that. I won't apologize. You can't mistreat people just because they're sick. They're still people, like anybody else. They have their rights.'

Silence.

'But if you think I'm some kind of spy or something, that I'm running around ratting on people to Ek—to Izmailova,

84

well that's simply not true. I mean, I talk to her, I'm not about to pretend I don't, but I'm not her spy or anything. She doesn't have any spies. She doesn't need any! She's just trying to hold things together, that's all.

'Jesus, you don't know what she's gone through for you! You haven't seen how much it takes out of her! She'd like nothing better than to quit. But she has to hang in there because—' An eerie dark electronic gabble rose up on his radio, and he stopped as he realized that they were laughing at him.

'Does anyone else wish to speak?'

One of Gunther's abductors stepped forward. 'Your Honour, this man says that flicks are human. He overlooks the fact that they cannot live without our support and direction. Their continued well-being is bought at the price of our unceasing labour. He stands condemned out of his own mouth. I petition the court to make the punishment fit the crime.'

The judge looked to the right, to the left. His two companions nodded, and stepped back into the void. The desk had been set up at the mouth of what was to be the air intake duct. Gunther had just time enough to realize this when they reappeared, leading someone in a G5 suit identical to his own.

'We could kill you, Mr Weil,' the artificial voice crackled. 'But that would be wasteful. Every hand, every mind is needed. We must all pull together in our time of need.'

The G5 suit stood alone and motionless in the centre of the room.

'Watch.'

Two of the Hyundai suits stepped up to the G5 suit. Four hands converged on the helmet seals. With practised efficiency, they flicked the latches and lifted the helmet. It happened so swiftly the occupant could not have stopped it if he'd tried.

Beneath the helmet was the fearful, confused face of a flick.

'Sanity is a privilege, Mr Weil, not a right. You are guilty as charged. However, we are not cruel men. *This once* we

85

will let you off with a warning. But these are desperate times. At your next offence – be it only so minor a thing as reporting this encounter to the Little General – we may be forced to dispense with the formality of a hearing.' The judge paused. 'Do I make myself clear?'

Reluctantly, Gunther nodded.

'Then you may leave.'

On the way out, one of the suits handed him back his peecee.

Five people. He was sure there weren't any more involved than that. Maybe one or two more, but that was it. Posner had to be hip-deep in this thing, he was certain of that. It shouldn't be too hard to figure out the others.

He didn't dare take the chance.

At shift's end he found Ekatarina already asleep. She looked haggard and unhealthy. He knelt by her, and gently brushed her cheek with the back of one hand.

Her eyelids fluttered open.

'Oh, hey. I didn't mean to wake you. Just go back to sleep, huh?'

She smiled. 'You're sweet, Gunther, but I was only taking a nap anyway. I've got to be up in another fifteen minutes.' Her eyes closed again. 'You're the only one I can really trust any more. Everybody's lying to me, feeding me misinformation, keeping silent when there's something I need to know. You're the only one I can count on to tell me things.'

You have enemies, he thought. They call you the Little General, and they don't like how you run things. They're not ready to move against you directly, but they have plans. And they're ruthless.

Aloud, he said, 'Go back to sleep.'

'They're all against me,' she murmured. 'Bastard sons of bitches.'

The next day he spent going through the service spaces for the new air-handling system. He found a solitary flick's nest made of shredded vacuum suits, but after consultation with the CMP concluded that nobody had lived there for days. There was no trace of Sally Chang.

If it had been harrowing going through the sealed areas before his trial, it was far worse today. Ekatarina's enemies had infected him with fear. Reason told him they were not waiting for him, that he had nothing to worry about until he displeased them again. But the hindbrain did not listen.

Time crawled. When he finally emerged into daylight at the end of his shift, he felt light-headedly out of phase with reality from the hours of isolation. At first he noticed nothing out of the ordinary. Then his suit radio was full of voices, and people were hurrying about every which way. There was a happy buzz in the air. Somebody was singing.

He snagged a passing suit and asked, 'What's going on?'

'Haven't you heard? The war is over. They've made peace. And there's a ship coming in!'

The *Lake Geneva* had maintained television silence through most of the long flight to the Moon for fear of long-range beam weapons. With peace, however, they opened direct transmission to Bootstrap.

Ezumi's people had the flicks sew together an enormous cotton square and hack away some trailing vines so they could hang it high on the shadowed side of the crater. Then, with the fill lights off, the video image was projected. Swiss spacejacks tumbled before the camera, grinning, all denim and red cowboy hats. They were talking about their escape from the hunter-seeker missiles, brash young voices running one over the other.

The top officers were assembled beneath the cotton square. Gunther recognized their suits. Ekatarina's voice boomed from newly erected loudspeakers. 'When are you coming in? We have to make sure the spaceport field is clear. How many hours?'

Holding up five fingers, a blonde woman said, 'Forty-five!'

'No, forty-three!'

'Nothing like that!'

'*Almost* forty-five!'

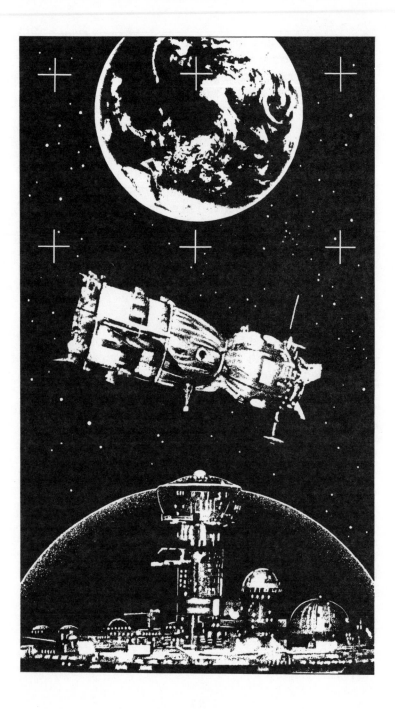

Again Ekatarina's voice cut into the tumult. 'What's it like in the orbitals? We heard they were destroyed.'

'Yes, destroyed!'

'Very bad, very bad, it'll take years to—'

'But most of the people are—'

'We were given six orbits' warning; most went down in lifting bodies – there was a big evacuation.'

'Many died, though. It was very bad.'

Just below the officers, a suit had been directing several flicks as they assembled a camera platform. Now it waved broadly, and the flicks stepped away. In the *Lake Geneva* somebody shouted, and several heads turned to stare at an offscreen television monitor. The suit turned the camera, giving them a slow, panoramic scan.

One of the spacejacks said, 'What's it like there? I see that some of you are wearing space suits, and the rest are not. Why is that?'

Ekatarina took a deep breath. 'There have been some changes here.'

There was one hell of a party at the Centre when the Swiss arrived. Sleep schedules were juggled, and save for a skeleton crew overseeing the flicks, everyone turned out to welcome the dozen newcomers to the Moon. They danced to skiffle, and drank vacuum-distilled vodka. Everyone had stories to tell, rumours to swap, opinions on the likelihood that the peace would hold.

Gunther wandered away midway through the party. The Swiss depressed him. They all seemed so young and fresh and eager. He felt battered and cynical in their presence. He wanted to grab them by the shoulders and shake them awake.

He wandered through the locked-down laboratories. Where the Viral Computer Project had been, he saw Ekatarina and the captain of the *Lake Geneva* conferring over a stack of crated bioflops. They bent low over Ekatarina's peecee, listening to the CMP.

'Have you considered nationalizing your industries?' the captain asked. 'That would give us the plant needed to build the New City. Then, with a few hardwired utilities, Bootstrap could be managed without anyone having to set foot inside it.'

Gunther was too distant to hear the CMP's reaction, but he saw both women laugh. 'Well,' said Ekatarina. 'At the very least we will have to renegotiate terms with the parent corporations. With only one ship functional, people can't be easily replaced. Physical presence has become a valuable commodity. We'd be fools not to take advantage of it.'

He passed on, deeper into shadow, wandering aimlessly. Eventually, there was a light ahead, and he heard voices. One was Krishna's, but spoken faster and more forcefully than he was used to hearing it. Curious, he stopped just outside the door.

Krishna was in the centre of the lab. Before him, Beth Hamilton stood nodding humbly. 'Yes, sir,' she said. 'I'll do that. Yes.' Dumbfounded, Gunther realized that Krishna was giving her orders.

Krishna glanced up. 'Weil! You're just the man I was about to come looking for.'

'I am?'

'Come in here, don't dawdle.' Krishna smiled and beckoned, and Gunther had no choice but to obey. He looked like a young god now. The force of his spirit danced in his eyes like fire. It was strange that Gunther had never noticed before how tall he was. 'Tell me where Sally Chang is.'

'I don't—I mean, I can't, I—' He stopped and swallowed. 'I think Chang must be dead.' Then, 'Krishna? What's happened to you?'

'He's finished his research,' Beth said.

'I rewrote my personality from top to bottom,' Krishna said. 'I'm not half-crippled with shyness any more – have you noticed?' He put a hand on Gunther's shoulder, and it was reassuring, warm, comforting. 'Gunther, I won't tell you what it took to scrape together enough messenger engines from traces of old experiments to try this out on myself. But it works. We've got a treatment that among other things will serve as a universal cure for everyone in

90

Bootstrap. But to do that, we need the messenger engines, and they're not here. Now tell me why you think Sally Chang is dead.'

'Well, uh, I've been searching for her for four days. And the CMP has been looking too. You've been holed up here all that time, so maybe you don't know the flicks as well as the rest of us do. But they're not very big on planning. The likelihood one of them could actively evade detection that long is practically zilch. The only thing I can think is that somehow she made it to the surface before the effects hit her, got into a truck and told it to drive as far as her oxygen would take her.'

Krishna shook his head and said, 'No. It is simply not consistent with Sally Chang's character. With all the best will in the world, I cannot picture her killing herself.' He slid open a drawer: row upon row of gleaming canisters. 'This may help. Do you remember when I said there were *two* canisters of mimetic engines missing, not just the schizo-mimetic?'

'Vaguely.'

'I've been too busy to worry about it, but wasn't that odd? Why would Chang have taken a canister and not used it?'

'What was in the second canister?' Hamilton asked.

'Paranoia,' Krishna said. 'Or rather a good enough chemical analogue. Now, paranoia is a rare disability, but a fascinating one. It's characterized by an elaborate but internally consistent delusional system. The paranoid patient functions well intellectually, and is less fragmented than a schizophrenic. Her emotional and social responses are closer to normal. She's capable of concerted effort. In a time of turmoil, it's quite possible that a paranoid individual could elude our detection.'

'Okay, let's get this straight,' Hamilton said. 'War breaks out on Earth. Chang gets her orders, keys in the software bombs, and goes to Bootstrap with a canister full of madness and a little syringe of paranoia – no, it doesn't work. It all falls apart.'

'How so?'

91

'Paranoia wouldn't inoculate her against schizophrenia. How does she protect herself from her own aerosols?'

Gunther stood transfixed. 'Lavender!'

They caught up with Sally Chang on the topmost terrace of Bootstrap. The top level was undeveloped. Someday – so the corporate brochures promised – fallow deer would graze at the edge of limpid pools, and otters frolic in the streams. But the soil hadn't been built up yet, the worms brought in or the bacteria seeded. There were only sand, machines, and a few unhappy opportunistic weeds.

Chang's camp was to one side of the streamhead, beneath a fill light. She started to her feet at their approach, glanced quickly to the side and decided to brazen it out.

A sign reading EMERGENCY CANOPY MAINTEN-ANCE STATION had been welded to a strut supporting the stream's valve stem. Under it were a short stacked pyramid of oxytanks and an aluminium storage crate the size of a coffin.

'Very clever,' Beth muttered over Gunther's trance chip. 'She sleeps in the storage crate, and anybody stumbling across her thinks it's just spare equipment.'

The lavender suit raised an arm and casually said, 'Hiya, guys. How can I help you?'

Krishna strode forward and took her hands. 'Sally, it's me – Krishna!'

'Oh, thank God!' She slumped in his arms. 'I've been so afraid.'

'You're all right now.'

'I though you were an Invader at first, when I saw you coming up. I'm so hungry – I haven't eaten since I don't know when.' She clutched at the sleeve of Krishna's suit. 'You do know about the Invaders, don't you?'

'Maybe you'd better bring me up to date.'

They began walking towards the stairs. Krishna gestured quietly to Gunther and then towards Chang's worksuit harness. A canister the size of a hip flask hung there. Gunther reached over and plucked it off. The messenger engines! He held them in his hand.

To the other side, Beth Hamilton plucked up the near-full cylinder of paranoia-inducing engines and made it disappear.

Sally Chang, deep in the explication of her reasonings, did not notice. ' . . . obeyed my orders, of course. But they made no sense. I worried and worried about that until finally I realized what was really going on. A wolf caught in a trap will gnaw off its leg to get free. I began to look for the wolf. What kind of enemy justified such extreme actions? Certainly nothing human.'

'Sally,' Krishna said, 'I want you to entertain the notion that the conspiracy – for want of a better word – may be more deeply rooted than you suspect. That the problem is not an external enemy, but the workings of our own brains. Specifically that the Invaders are an artifact of the psychoto-mimetics you injected into yourself back when this all began.'

'No. No, there's too much evidence. It all fits together! The Invaders needed a way to disguise themselves both physically, which was accomplished by the vacuum suits, and psychologically, which was achieved by the general madness. Thus, they can move undetected among us. Would a human enemy have converted all of Bootstrap to slave labour? Unthinkable! They can read our minds like a book. If we hadn't protected ourselves with the schizo-mimetics, they'd be able to extract all our knowledge, all our military research secrets . . .'

Listening, Gunther couldn't help imagining what Liza Nagenda would say to all of this wild talk. At the thought of her, his jaw clenched. Just like one of Chang's machines, he realized, and couldn't help being amused at his own expense.

Ekatarina was waiting at the bottom of the stairs. Her hands trembled noticeably, and there was a slight quaver in her voice when she said, 'What's all this the CMP tells me about messenger engines? Krishna's supposed to have come up with a cure of some kind?'

'We've got them,' Gunther said quietly, happily. He held up the canister. 'It's over now, we can heal our friends.'

'Let me see,' Ekatarina said. She took the canister from his hand.

'No, wait!' Hamilton cried, too late. Behind her, Krishna was arguing with Sally Chang about her interpretations of recent happenings. Neither had noticed yet that those in front had stopped.

'Stand back.' Ekatarina took two quick steps backward. Edgily, she added, 'I don't mean to be difficult. But we're going to sort this all out, and until we do, I don't want anybody too close to me. That includes you too, Gunther.'

Flicks began gathering. By ones and twos they wandered up the lawn, and then by the dozen. By the time it was clear that Ekatarina had called them up via the CMP, Krishna, Chang and Hamilton were separated from her and Gunther by a wall of people.

Chang stood very still. Somewhere behind her unseen face, she was revising her theories to include this new event. Suddenly, her hands slapped at her suit, grabbing for the missing canisters. She looked at Krishna and with a trill of horror said, 'You're one of them!'

'Of course I'm not—' Krishna began. But she was turning, stumbling, fleeing back up the steps.

'Let her go,' Ekatarina ordered. 'We've got more serious things to talk about.' Two flicks scurried up, lugging a small industrial kiln between them. They set it down, and a third plugged in an electric cable. The interior began to glow. 'This canister is all you've got, isn't it? If I were to autoclave it, there wouldn't be any hope of replacing its contents.'

'Izmailova, listen,' Krishna said.

'I am listening. Talk.'

Krishna explained, while Izmailova listened with arms folded and shoulders tilted sceptically. When he was done, she shook her head. 'It's a noble folly, but folly is all it is. You want to reshape our minds into something alien to the course of human evolution. To turn the seat of thought into a jet pilot's couch. This is your idea of a solution? Forget it. Once this particular box is opened, there'll be no putting its contents back in again. And you haven't advanced any convincing arguments for opening it.'

'But the people in Bootstrap!' Gunther objected. 'They—'

She cut him off. 'Gunther, nobody *likes* what's happened to them. But if the rest of us must give up our humanity to pay for a speculative and ethically dubious rehabilitation ... Well, the price is simply too high. Mad or not, they're at least human now.'

'Am I inhuman?' Krishna asked. 'If you tickle me, do I not laugh?'

'You're in no position to judge. You've rewired your neurons and you're stoned on the novelty. What tests have you run on yourself? How thoroughly have you mapped out your deviations from human norms? Where are your figures?' These were purely rhetorical questions; the kind of analyses she meant took weeks to run. 'Even if you check out completely human – and I don't concede you will! – who's to say what the long-range consequences are? What's to stop us from drifting, step by incremental step, into madness? Who decides what madness is? Who programs the programmers? No, this is impossible. I won't gamble with our minds.' Defensively, almost angrily, she repeated, 'I won't gamble with our minds.'

'Ekatarina,' Gunther said gently, 'how long have you been up? Listen to yourself. The wire is doing your thinking for you.'

She waved a hand dismissively, without responding.

'Just as a practical matter,' Hamilton said, 'how do you expect to run Bootstrap without it? The setup now is turning us all into baby fascists. You say you're worried about madness – what will we be like a year from now?'

'The CMP assures me—'

'The CMP is only a program!' Hamilton cried. 'No matter how much interactivity it has, it's not flexible. It has no hope. It cannot judge a new thing. It can only enforce old decisions, old values, old habits, old fears.'

Abruptly Ekatarina snapped. *'Get out of my face!'* she screamed. 'Stop it, stop it, stop it! I won't listen to any more.'

'Ekatarina—' Gunther began.

But her hand had tightened on the canister. Her knees bent as she began a slow genuflection to the kiln. Gunther could see that she had stopped listening. Drugs and responsibility had done this to her, speeding her up and bewildering her with conflicting demands, until she stood trembling on the brink of collapse. A good night's sleep might have restored her, made her capable of being reasoned with. But there was no time. Words would not stop her now. And she was too far distant for him to reach before she destroyed the engines. In that instant he felt such a strong outwelling of emotion towards her as would be impossible to describe.

'Ekatarina,' he said. 'I love you.'

She half-turned her head towards him and in a distracted, somewhat irritated tone said, 'What are you—'

He lifted the bolt gun from his work harness, levelled it, and fired.

Ekatarina's helmet shattered.

She fell.

'I should have shot to just breach the helmet. That would have stopped her. But I didn't think I was a good enough shot. I aimed right for the centre of her head.'

'Hush,' Hamilton said. 'You did what you had to. Stop tormenting yourself. Talk about more practical things.'

He shook his head, still groggy. For the longest time, he had been kept on beta endorphins, unable to feel a thing, unable to care. It was like being swathed in cotton batting. Nothing could reach him. Nothing could hurt him. 'How long have I been out of it?'

'A day.'

'A day!' He looked about the austere room. Bland rock walls and laboratory equipment with smooth, noncommittal surfaces. To the far end, Krishna and Chang were hunched over a swipeboard, arguing happily and impatiently overwriting each other's scrawls. A Swiss spacejack came in and spoke to their backs. Krishna nodded distractedly, not looking up. 'I thought it was much longer.'

'Long enough. We've already salvaged everyone connected with Sally Chang's group, and gotten a good start on the rest. Pretty soon it will be time to decide how you want yourself rewritten.'

He shook his head, feeling dead. 'I don't think I'll bother, Beth. I just don't have the stomach for it.'

'We'll give you the stomach.'

'Naw, I don't . . .' He felt a black nausea come welling up again. It was cyclic; it returned every time he was beginning to think he'd finally put it down. 'I don't want the fact that I killed Ekatarina washed away in a warm flood of self-satisfaction. The idea disgusts me.'

'We don't want that either.' Posner led a delegation of seven into the lab. Krishna and Chang rose to face them, and the group broke into swirling halves. 'There's been enough of that. It's time we all started taking responsibility for the consequences of—' Everyone was talking at once. Hamilton made a face.

'Started taking responsibility for—'

Voices rose.

'We can't talk here,' she said 'Take me out on the surface.'

They drove with the cabin pressurized, due west on the Seething Bay road. Ahead, the sun was almost touching the weary walls of Sömmering crater. Shadow crept down from the mountains and cratertops, yearning towards the radiantly lit Sinus Medii. Gunther found it achingly beautiful. He did not want to respond to it, but the harsh lines echoed the lonely hurt within him in a way that he found oddly comforting.

Hamilton touched her peecee. 'Putting on the Ritz' filled their heads.

'What if Ekatarina was right?' he said sadly. 'What if we're giving up everything that makes us human? The prospect of being turned into some kind of big-domed emotionless superman doesn't appeal to me much.'

Hamilton shook her head. 'I asked Krishna about that, and he said No. He said it was like . . . Were you ever nearsighted?'

'Sure, as a kid.'

'Then you'll understand. He said it was like the first time you came out of the doctor's office after being lased. How everything seemed clear and vivid and distinct. What had once been a blur that you called "tree" resolved itself into a thousand individual and distinct leaves. The world was filled with unexpected detail. There were things on the horizon that you'd never seen before. Like that.'

'Oh.' He stared ahead. The disc of the sun was almost touching Sömmering. 'There's no point in going any farther.'

He powered down the truck.

Beth Hamilton looked uncomfortable. She cleared her throat and with brusque energy said, 'Gunther, look. I had you bring me out here for a reason. I want to propose a merger of resources.'

'A what?'

'Marriage.'

It took Gunther a second to absorb what she had said. 'Aw, no . . . I don't . . .'

'I'm serious. Gunther, I know you think I've been hard on you, but that's only because I saw a lot of potential in you, and that you were doing nothing with it. Well, things have changed. Give me a say in your rewrite, and I'll do the same for you.'

He shook his head. 'This is just too weird for me.'

'It's too late to use that as an excuse. Ekatarina was right – we're sitting on top of something very dangerous, the most dangerous opportunity humanity faces today. It's out of the bag, though. Word has gotten out. Earth is horrified and fascinated. They'll be watching us. Briefly, very briefly, we can control this thing. We can help to shape it now, while it's small. Five years from now, it will be out of our hands.

'You have a good mind, Gunther, and it's about to get better. I think we agree on what kind of a world we want to make. I want you on my side.'

'I don't know what to say.'

'You want true love? You got it. We can make the sex as

99

sweet or nasty as you like. Nothing easier. You want me quieter, louder, gentler, more assured? We can negotiate. Let's see if we can come to terms.'

He said nothing.

Hamilton eased back in the seat. After a time, she said, 'You know? I've never watched a lunar sunset before. I don't get out on the surface much.'

'We'll have to change that,' Gunther said.

Hamilton stared hard into his face. Then she smiled. She wriggled closer to him. Clumsily, he put an arm over her shoulder. It seemed to be what was expected of him. He coughed into his hand, then pointed a finger. 'There it goes.'

Lunar sunset was a simple thing. The crater wall touched the bottom of the solar disc. Shadows leaped from the slopes and raced across the lowlands. Soon half the sun was gone. Smoothly, without distortion, it dwindled. A last brilliant sliver of light burned atop the rock, then ceased to be. In the instant before the windshield adjusted and the stars appeared, the universe filled with darkness.

The air in the cab cooled. The panels snapped and popped with the sudden shift in temperature.

Now Hamilton was nuzzling the side of his neck. Her skin was slightly tacky to the touch, and exuded a faint but distinct odour. She ran her tongue up the line of his chin and poked it in his ear. Her hand fumbled with the latches of his suit.

Gunther experienced no arousal at all, only a mild distaste that bordered on disgust. This was horrible, a defilement of all he had felt for Ekatarina.

But it was a chore he had to get through. Hamilton was right. All his life his hindbrain had been in control, driving him with emotions chemically derived and randomly applied. He had been lashed to the steed of consciousness and forced to ride it wherever it went, and that nightmare gallop had brought him only pain and confusion. Now that he had control of the reins, he could make this horse go where he wanted.

He was not sure what he would demand from his repro-

100

gramming. Contentment, perhaps. Sex and passion, almost certainly. But not love. He was done with the romantic delusion. It was time to grow up.

He squeezed Beth's shoulder. One more day, he thought, and it won't matter. I'll feel whatever is best for me to feel. Beth raised her mouth to his. Her lips parted. He could smell her breath.

They kissed.